THE LONG ROPE

THE LONG ROPE

Francis W. Hilton

GUNSMOKE

This hardback edition 2009
by BBC Audiobooks Ltd
by arrangement with
Golden West Literary Agency

ISBN 978 1 405 68237 4

British Library Cataloguing in Publication Data available.

Printed and bound in Great Britain by
CPI Antony Rowe, Chippenham, Wiltshire

THE LONG ROPE

List of Chapters—

"Stop that fellow! He's done murder!" Peep O'Day plunges away from the Jumbo Saloon—a fugitive from the law.

The Long Rope

Chapter One

Brothers in Name Only

Squealing, biting, kicking, a herd of horses thundered down from Ragged Hound Butte. They took the steep, grottoed bank into Surprise Creek on their rumps, bunched quickly, and strung out up the trail in a long, swiftly moving column. Behind bobbed two riders—mere corks on a swimming sea of heat. Alkali dust hung in a murky cloud along the back trail. Dust rose chokingly from the greasewood flats to powder their chaps and wide-brimmed hats and glisten in the stubble on their faces, grim and hard in the glare of the summer sun blazing a downward path through coppery skies to the horizon. Dust hung to their sticky saddles and lay in a gray blanket on the sweaty necks of their mounts.

A third rider kept to the rim of the cutbank above. With slicing rowels he goaded his horse to a mad gallop in an attempt to outrun the racing herd. But the pony's action was jerky, mechanical—the movements of a brute leg-weary from long miles on the trail, wilted by a blasting sun.

Where Surprise Creek narrowed suddenly into a blind ravine the brute took a deep dry wash in a bound, cut in ahead, and pounded on toward a cottonwood pole corral, ears plastered hatefully, bloody froth flying from distended muzzle, dust-rimmed eyes gleaming malevolently.

Gaining the enclosure, the rider set the brute onto its haunches, leaped down, dropped the poles, and vaulted back into the saddle just as the herd popped up out of the creek bed to come on a dead run.

With shouts, curses, and waving arms the trio succeeded

in turning the snorting, wild-eyed animals, which, with burr-matted tails straight out like rudders, strove with savage glee to break through the cordon. Of a sudden the leader, a star-faced sorrel with finely chiseled head, broad intelligent forehead, and deep barrel, slid to a halt on trim, spraddled legs and minced warily into the corral. The others whirled, quieted, and followed meekly.

Once the herd was inside, the first rider, Jim Thompson, owner of the big T-7 outfit, again swung down.

"There's that star-faced Torpedo hellion that killed you kids' paw," he announced, replacing the peeled poles to bar the entrance.

A giant of a man was Thompson, with great broad shoulders, slightly stooped, massive thighs, and muscular arms that dangled to his knees. He hoisted brush-scarred chaps with his wrists, pushed back a dusty hat to run horny fingers through matted damp gray hair and brush it away from a corrugated, sweat-beaded brow. He straightened up to face his two companions.

"Climb in there, Peep," he boomed to his young foreman, Peep O'Day. "Toss a rope onto Torpedo so we can turn the rest of the hellions loose. We've gaunted them up a-plenty for one day, short as our water supply is. And we'll be needing every head of them for cavvy strings pronto. You, Tommy," he threw at the other of the two, something of a smile lighting his ugly, weather-whipped features and faded brown eyes and quirking the corners of thick, wind-cracked lips, "I reckon your paw left you the job of tromping Torpedo down."

Without comment the youth addressed as Peep unbuckled his throw rope and dismounted. The movement was easy, graceful, suggestive of the catlike quickness of a puma.

The other, Tommy O'Day, Peep's brother, shook a booted foot free from a sweaty stirrup, slapped savagely at his shying mount, and crooked a chapped leg about a dancing saddle-horn, fanning himself with his hat to stir up the air that hung inert and suffocating over the shimmering flats.

"I don't see just why I've been elected to get revenge on that snake-eyed sorrel for killing Paw," he returned sullenly. "I'll do the roping, if you'll fork him, Peep."

Having ground-picketed his lathering horse, which shifted its weight on three legs to blow furiously, Peep whirled out the kinks from his throw rope.

"Yaller?" he asked quietly.

Tommy's foot found the stirrup. He snapped straight in his saddle, jerked down his hat to shield eyes suddenly lighted with points of flame.

Thompson intercepted the hot retort that sprang to his lips.

"I don't blame you, Tommy—or any other jasper, for showing yaller when it comes to tying into this man-killer," the cowman soothed. "I'm sure glad forking him wasn't wished off onto me." He pulled his huge bulk into the saddle and neck-reined about. "But ride the hellion or kill him as far as I'm concerned. I'll just take a *pasear* up along the head of the creek yonder and pick up that bunch of yearlings. I'll be back in an hour or so. Then we'll mosey on toward the ranch."

The two watched him in silence as he galloped away, his huge body glued to the saddle, his great arms flapping like the wings of a crane. When he had dipped from sight in a dry wash, Peep turned back to the sullen Tommy.

"Paw left you the job of tromping Torpedo down," he reminded in a tone that stung with its quietness. "I'd bust him if it was the last thing I ever did on earth."

His cool, gray eyes shifted from the plainly uneasy Tommy to the corral in which, but a month before, Hank O'Day, their father, had made his last ride on the star-faced sorrel which now stood, legs spraddled wide, peeking at them through the poles with glazed, scheming eyes.

"You're brave as the devil as long as you didn't have the job wished off on you, ain't you?" Tommy sneered.

He swung down, unbuckled and jerked loose his lariat, stamped over to the corral, and crawled between the poles. His movements were quick, nervous, reflecting the boiling anger that possessed him. He whirled out his noose savagely. The singing rope set the animals to running around him.

When the brutes had circled the corral at a gallop a half-dozen times, churning dust that swirled upward in choking clouds to settle back in a thin gray film on greasewood and sage, Tommy leaped in front of them. They broke wildly about him.

Singling out the star-faced sorrel, he whipped his noose back across his shoulder. It snapped forward with the speed of a striking snake and circled the animal's neck. Quicker even than the lunge Torpedo made on the rope was Tommy's own move as he bounded over and took a dally around the worn cottonwood snubbing-post in the center of the corral. Then he sprang from range of the hoofs of the outlaw, which had whirled and started for him, squealing ferociously, teeth bared, front legs flailing the air.

Peep leaped over to the bars and dropped them. The rest of the horses bolted outside, crowding, snorting, rocking the corral poles in their mad scramble to escape. When they finally had succeeded in jamming through the gate, and had run off in half circles to look back inquisitively, Peep replaced the poles and strode in to where the straining Tommy was slowly dragging the infuriated sorrel up to the snubbing-post.

"That's the ticket, kid," Peep said admiringly. "I knew you'd do it."

"Like hell I will," Tommy retorted savagely. "I wouldn't step across that hellion after the way he killed Paw if he was broke to the plow. I don't see any reason for me getting my neck kinked just because Paw got a fool notion he wanted me to clean up on this man-killing devil."

Peep stopped stock still to whip amazed gray eyes along his brother's taut figure. Although the two, with their clear-cut, deeply tanned features, broad shoulders, and slender hips, were as alike as twins in appearance, they were the antithesis of one another in character. No one knew better than the taciturn, even-tempered, deep-thinking Peep the vast difference between them.

Since childhood Tommy had run a course as wild and unbridled as that of any outlaw on the Satanka range. He had been the idol of his father, Hank O'Day, who laughed at his escapades and took secret delight in his recklessness. Time and again the level-headed Peep—who had known no childhood, but had, since his earliest recollection, been doing the work of a range-hand—remonstrated with old Hank. To no avail. Tommy's glib tongue was always sufficient to win any argument; his hair-trigger temper and sullen anger always reared up, a successful barrier to reason as a last resort.

As a result, the shiftless, selfish youth had come to the threshold of manhood filled with an exaggerated idea of his own importance, a ruthless disregard for the rights of others, possessed of a cocksureness that was little short of unbearable. He was too unreliable to hold a position of trust, too lazy and restless to stick to any sort of work for any length of time. He had become a range drifter, at present riding for the T-7, although it galled him deeply to take orders from the close-lipped, determined Peep, Jim Thompson's foreman.

Conscientious to an amazing degree, possessed of a loyalty to trust that was little short of a mania, the quick-moving, confident Peep was a stickler for duty, a tireless worker, a man who put his heart and soul into any task no matter how menial. His word was his bond. Everyone called him friend, respected him. Yet that respect was tempered with a certain amount of fear and something of awe. For the steely-eyed, taciturn youth invited no intimates, brooked no interference in anything he was about.

The last whispered plea their dying father had made, to look out for Tommy, had become a solemn duty to Peep. He had tried patiently to curb his headstrong brother. But his approach was blunt and tactless. Tommy only flew into a rage and refused to listen.

There in the corral at the head of Surprise Creek, that blistering August day, the silence between the two deepened, suddenly became strained. Tommy gave vent to his boiling rage by savagely sawing on the rope and dragging the outlaw up to the snubbing-post. By now the brute's breath was rasping croupily in its throat. Its wide-spraddled forelegs were trembling violently. Lower and lower it sank as it was reeled in by the burning rope that cut at its windpipe. Finally, choked down, it sat on its haunches, dropped heavily to the ground.

Without a word, Peep spun about and crawled from the corral. He returned presently with his saddle, which he had stripped from the steaming back of his mount outside.

"Tommy," he pleaded, as he worked his way, hand over hand, along the taut rope to the side of the groaning outlaw, "why don't you come down off your high horse and be pards with me, like Paw asked? He gave us a good start in the Flying Spear. With the money he said was in the bank at Satanka we can buy a few more head of cows and cut the riffle together in great shape. We're sitting on top of the world together—"

"With you riding herd on me all the time?" Tommy stopped him sneeringly. "With you always claiming I'm shiftless and hotheaded, always trying to make a bell-ewe out of me? Not on your life. If you'll ever go to town and split the money Paw left us I'll have something to start out with on my own hook. You take the Flying Spear and go to hell with it. I want to see something besides these damned blistered flats, smell something besides stinking greasewood and burned cow hair, hear something— But most of all I'm sick and tired of your damned preaching."

A sudden tensing of the muscles at the corners of his set jaws was the only indication Peep gave that he even heard the furious outburst. He deftly knotted a hackamore and worked it over the snapping jaws of the fallen outlaw.

"Damned if I'd treat him so gentle," Tommy sneered, obviously bent on angering his brother. "I'd put a war-bridle on that man-killing hellion and tear the jaws plumb off him."

"I never saw any dumb brute I got pleasure in torturing, no matter what it had done," Peep flashed back scathingly. "This here Torpedo is a fighter, that's all. Just like lots of men. He isn't to blame. It's born in some horses just like it is in some men. War-bridle, hell. We'll fight him clean with a hackamore, give him a gambling chance. Then if he gets us—"

He straightened up, wiped the trickling sweat from his grimy face with the back of his hand, and searched in the trouser pockets beneath his brush-scarred chaps, presently to pull forth a bandanna, which he tucked into the hackamore across the white-rimmed eyes.

"I wonder just what Paw was thinking when he died!" he mused grimly as he set to work again rigging up the outlaw that threshed about wildly on the ground. "He gave me his forty-one Colt when he knew I hadn't packed a gun for five years and never could stay out of trouble when I toted one. He gave you his saddle when he knew you didn't have the guts to straddle a pair of bars and rake 'em clean. And his hair rope—the finest and longest rope that ever came into these parts—he gave you that rope knowing you were the best roper on the Satanka. Didn't it ever strike you kind of funny, Tommy? You don't suppose Paw was deliberately putting temptation in our way, do you?" He jerked slack in the taut lariat.

Torpedo sucked his lungs full of air, struggled to his feet. Tommy let the brute get up, then snubbed him closer. Torpedo made a few wild lunges, fighting his head, throwing his body. Then he quieted down cunningly—as though saving his strength—only sagged in the middle as Peep eased the saddle onto his back. Blinded, he made no attempt to renew the fight, but stood spread-legged with his weight against the choking rope, steel-banded muscles bulging.

"How the devil can I help it if I'm no rider," Tommy blurted out bitterly. "I'll swap Paw's saddle for that forty-one Colt he gave you any old time. I reckon I can handle that—and this rope, even if I can't—"

"Would you part with what Paw gave you?" Peep demanded, fishing warily beneath the brute's belly for the dangling latigo. Catching it, he placed a booted foot against Torpedo's suddenly swollen side, and despite the savage kicking of the brute, jerked it to the last notch.

"Sure." Tommy answered the question shortly. "I never had nothing I wouldn't sell or trade if I got my price. Why not?"

"Nothing." Peep stepped back from the groaning outlaw. "Well, there you are. After a month of chasing there's old Torpedo r'aring and snorting to go places. Paw gave him to you providing you'd tromp hell out of him. If you couldn't, he asked you to pass him along to the jasper who could. One of us is going to fork him here and now."

"Honest, Peep, I just haven't the heart since I saw him—since he killed Paw," Tommy blurted out nervously. "Besides, I don't want him. You can have the ornery devil if—"

Peep stepped back from range of the wicked hoofs, slapping viciously at the cinch, to tighten his spur straps.

"Crawfishing out of this just like you've crawfished out of everything hard and unpleasant all your life, aren't you, Tommy?" he remarked caustically. "You're yaller—yaller from your innards clean to your hide. But let me tell you something." He jerked straight, his gray eyes glinting like burnished steel, his mouth a thin grim slit. "I'll make this ride for you—like I've done everything else for you that's hard ever since you were knee-high to a grasshopper. But after this, I'm through. I'm not going to let you duck out of things like Paw did. He made me swear I'd look out for you. He died thinking you were a man. And, by God, I'll make a man out of you or give up the ghost trying. You might as well lope along up yonder and help Jim gather those yearlings. I don't need you here any longer."

Making the outlaw fast to the snubbing-post, Tommy strode from the corral. Without a word he slammed into his saddle, lifted his horse with a savage jab of the rowels, and galloped away. Not once did he look back.

Peep did not notice. He calmly took over the lariat, loosened it, slipped it from Torpedo's neck. The muscles of the hand that gripped the hackamore rope were bloodless. In a single leap he too was in the saddle, had settled himself and found the stirrups. Leaning over, he stripped off the blind.

"Do your damnedest," he rasped out through set teeth. "You've killed one O'Day and made a coward out of another. There are only three of us and, by God, here's where either you or me break our picks. Unlimber and untwist, you hellion, for we're going—"

His spur rowels sank home. His quirt raised a livid welt on a violently quivering shoulder.

Chapter Two

Tromping Down an Outlaw

Stark terror rooted Torpedo in his tracks for a moment. Then the wild hot blood of outlawry surging through his veins goaded him to action. A snort of defiance whistled through his flaring nostrils. A bawl, not unlike the challenge of an enraged bull, rumbled in his throat, burst with terrifying shrillness. A quick jerk on the hackamore rope and his nose was threaded between his fetlocks. His great humped body bowed into a clevis, a clevis white-hot with rage, braced with muscles of steel. He whipped out as though from a catapult. His flashing belly half-turned to the brassy sky. He landed with a sickening wrench, a stone-crusher in front, double-barreled, deadly behind. He stood quivering for a clock-tick, aimed a vicious kick at a gouging rowel. Then he was gone again, bawling raucously, his body a bundle of mighty spring coils, whipping, twisting, writhing, pivoting. Straight for the corral poles he went, lurching against them in a cunning attempt to scrape Peep's leg from the stirrup.

"Naw you don't," the grim-lipped youth taunted. "You'll snag yourself before you get me that way. Give me what you've got and let's get it over with. 'Cause it's you or me." The quirt raised another long livid welt on the sweaty shoulder. A rowel opened a gash in a heaving side.

Torpedo faltered for an instant. Fear drove the murderous glaze from white-rimmed eyes. One hatefully plastered ear joined its fellow straight out in front. The sound of that voice, cool and unafraid, heightened the terror born of the slashing rowels and burning quirt. This adversary was far superior to others he had taken down to defeat. This rider, for all his bloodless face and quick, catlike movements that instilled fear in man and beast, was raking those flesh-searing rowels from his neck to his rump. Something the others had not dared do. And that quirt— It was paralyzing his shoulder, filling him with maddening pain. Instinct warned him that this battle would be different from those others.

He summoned every ounce of his prodigious strength for the next lightning leap. He went high, sunfished his belly to the sky, came down with his rump where his nose had started. The knee clamp above only tightened until it seemed his sides would cave with the pressure.

The searing pain of those sharp rowels goaded him on. Pain in his shoulder turned him into a demon, frothing at the mouth, bawling wildly, determined to crush the life from his terrifying opponent or die in the attempt.

Brain against brawn. Torpedo didn't know the meaning of brain, but he was using every ounce of his brawn. His instinct told him now that for all his inherent cunning, for all his primitive, unmastered outlawry, he was waging a losing battle. But fighter that he was—

He popped skyward, landed with a sickening wrench that made his own bones pop. Up on his hind legs he came, poised until it seemed the slow hot wind whining in the coulees would topple him backward. He was losing balance, going over. Then—

The loaded end of the stinging quirt left a knot between his ears. He came down on all fours, straightened out, shaking his head savagely. That bruised head dropped back between his fetlocks. But its movement now was neither fast nor terrifying.

Occasionally Peep was forced to stop punishing the brute to regain his own balance. Dogged determination supplied the knee grip necessary to stay on the writhing, twisting back. His joints ached with the merciless wrenching. His head had whipped until it was spinning and seemed disjointed from his body. But he hung on. Each time the brute lunged he caught a glimpse of a wildly whirling world far beneath. Again he was looking up into a sky that glittered like a sheet of tin before his aching eyes. The corral itself was spinning like a merry-go-round. Dust eddied upward in suffocating sheets. With every clock-tick the blazing sun grew more torrid. Perspiration ran in rivulets down his grimy face, trickled off his nose, and stung his bloodshot eyes. Even the breeze that now whipped his hair was sickening with heat, the odor of sweaty flesh, of blistered greasewood and fennel.

But his lips were still braced in a thin, grim line. His lean jaw bulged with the pressure of clamped teeth. The fighting face of Peep O'Day—a replica of the face of old Hank, who but a month before in that same corral, aboard that same outlaw had—

Pains began shooting through Peep's legs. His brain took to reeling drunkenly. His faculties seemed numbed. His battered muscles rebelled at further punishment. Yet he managed to keep those knees clamped, managed to keep the rowels slashing and the quirt descending to bring blood popping from livid welts. Instinctively he knew, as did the outlaw beneath him, that here was a fight to the finish, a relentless battle without mercy or quarter.

One by one Torpedo exhausted his store of tricks. Then on Peep's numbed brain burst the realization that the brute was weakening. It lent him strength, gave him renewed vigor for the fray. Reaching down, he stripped off the hackamore, lashed Torpedo across the rump with it. This unprecedented bit of daring threw the brute into a new frenzy. His stiff-legged jolts increased in violence, brought blood gushing from Peep's nose. The youth shook it out of his eyes, redoubled his efforts to conquer the sorrel before his own battered body gave out under the terrific abuse.

But the legs that now threw the rowels into the heaving

sides were logy with fatigue. The arm that had wielded the quirt could scarcely lift the hackamore to lay it across the lather-smeared rump. Man and horse alike were unsteady with weariness, wilted with their efforts beneath the blasting sun.

The indomitable will of the clinging human, who defied his greatest and most cunning tricks, undermined the courage of Torpedo and gradually took the fight out of him.

He made a few more half-hearted lunges. Then he stopped—stopped to stand spread-legged, trembling like a newborn colt, crushed, bruised, beaten, sweat oozing in dirty lather from beneath the saddle, dripping from his quivering belly. Too spent to resist, he only grunted under the rowels and craned a neck to stare dully at the boot gouging at his side.

After a final futile attempt to budge the animal, Peep swung down and attempted to leap from range of the deadly hoofs. But his own legs had become tallow, would scarcely support his weight. He lurched drunkenly to Torpedo's head. The outlaw jerked back, glowering through sweat-rimmed eyes. The snort it essayed was but a wheeze through distended, heaving nostrils from which trickled blood. But the spark of outlawry still pulsing through its veins curled its upper lip.

Torpedo bundled his logy muscles to charge, strike, beat down this tormentor as he had beaten down others. But instead of fleeing, as those others had done, this man had calmly reached out and was scratching his bloody muzzle. Instinctively conscious of an overwhelming sense of relief that he was not called upon to renew the grueling fight, the sorrel relaxed. Taut muscles fell to quivering with renewed violence. The curl left its lip. It took a step forward on unsteady legs, rubbed its frothy muzzle and bruised ears against Peep's arm.

"There you are, Paw," the youth breathed reverently.

"I've tromped him down like you asked. He was a killer. But he wasn't to blame. We ought to blame the fellow who tried to break him in the first place."

Even the youth's panting voice had lost its terror for Torpedo. Somehow, now, it was soothing and inspired confidence. Here was a man who he knew instinctively meant him no harm. Unlike the others who had abused and mistreated him, this man had only proved his mastery and now was offering friendship.

"Reckon now you've taken your licking like a sport, we'll be friends," Torpedo heard the voice saying in a soothing friendly fashion. "I've whipped you down, so cut out the foolishness. But I'm not fooling you any, fellow, you gave me the dangedest bone-cracking I ever got on any horse in any round corral."

Torpedo could only twist his weary head and blow frantically to fill his bursting lungs with air. But he liked that voice, liked the fearlessness of this man who coolly reknotted the hackamore about his rope-burned jaws, uncinched the saddle and dragged it from his reeking back. Time was when he would have shied violently as the leather hit the ground. But somehow he had neither the spirit nor the urge to lunge away.

Wearily Peep took the hair rope from the snubbing-post, coiled it with practiced hands. The hair rope their father had given Tommy!

"No better rope ever came into any cow country." The cracked, weak voice of their dying father seemed to come again from somewhere on the blistered flats just outside the corral. "You'll always know it, 'cause it's got a streak of yaller braided into it. That rope has steered clear of critters that didn't belong to our little Flying Spear spread, kids. It's yours now, Tommy. Take care of it. And swear to me you'll never toss it on anything that don't belong to you."

Jerking himself violently from his bitter retrospection,

Peep buckled the coiled rope onto his saddle. This done, he shouldered the saddle and went outside to rig up his horse, which, with bridle reins trailing, had left off grazing to peek inquisitively through the poles at the foam-splattered and thoroughly subdued Torpedo. Dropping the bars, Peep swung up, rode back, and secured the hackamore rope. As the lead rope grew tight, the outlaw planted its front feet and crowded back, rump against the poles, throwing its body violently, fore-hoofs slapping the ground, fighting its head savagely. Half-hearted bawls escaped its curled lip.

Looping a dally around the saddlehorn, the youth touched his mount lightly with his bloody, hair-matted rowels. The horse, a master of the snubbing-rope, lunged. Torpedo came up straight, but with legs spraddled. For all his violent head-shaking and determined resistance he was dragged outside the corral, fore-hoofs plowing furrows in the earth. There, bested at every turn, he calmed down and sidled up to rub bruised jaws against the flank of Peep's pony.

Once he had the animal outside, Peep shifted sidewise in his stirrups and swept the shimmering flats for sight of Thompson and Tommy. Not locating them immediately and content to rest after the grueling fight, he fell to an idle survey of the country, a region of brush-clotted flats, gashed with writhing washes. Here and there a gnarled cottonwood tree held a promise of water, a promise that was not fulfilled by the dusty, bone-dry creek beds. Beyond, the Ragged Hound buttes reared their ugly helms, gumbo sides gray, corrugated, suggesting white-hot metal that has burst its mold and cooled as it ran. It was a region uninviting, a region dotted with scraggly, dusty vegetation and cured forage, awesome in its vastness, scourged by the sun and blistering breeze that whined dismally in the coulees.

Two miles down the valley of Surprise Creek the few

squatty shacks of the Flying Spear danced like a mirage in the heat that rose in shimmering waves from the griddle-hot prairies. Beyond the Flying Spear, the big T-7 spread out like a miniature city. Cleaving its pastures, the Belle Fourche River sparkled, a ribbon of blinding brilliance, twisting into the meadowlands—the one spot of green on the whole drab expanse. Glistening barbed-wire fences slashed the haze like fingers of flame. The horizon was but a faint blue etching, unreal, ever-changing.

Rested, after a time, Peep again shifted his weary weight in the saddle and pulled his gaze from the dismal view.

"I've done part of what you wanted, Paw," he muttered aloud, as he wiped the sweat from his grimy face. "I've topped Torpedo and blistered him. I didn't mind that. You can beat some sense into a good horse even if he is an outlaw. And I'll do my best on that other job you gave me. But I sure wish you hadn't asked me to look out for Tommy."

Once again he settled down, lost in thought that took no notice of time. The steel-gray eyes that roved the flats now saw nothing. Not until his pony whinnied and he sighted the trail dust of the oncoming yearlings did he rouse himself. Then, dragging the sullen Torpedo along, he rode forth to meet Thompson and Tommy. His approach was unnoticed. The two were in deep conversation that stopped abruptly as he came up.

Chapter Three

LONG-ROPE SWINGERS

PEEP'S FEAT OF HORSEMANSHIP in mastering the man-killer Torpedo made him the hero of the hour on the Satanka range. When he rode into the T-7 that evening, the thoroughly cowed and leg-weary outlaw snubbed to his saddle horn, there was even greater respect in the eyes of the punchers, something akin to awe. That Peep had had the temerity to "tromp down" the brute—the terror of the range—filled them with admiration. Especially was that true in view of the fact that Torpedo had killed the youth's father. By all the unwritten laws of rangeland that should have made the animal the young foreman's "jinx hoss." For punchers since time immemorial have been superstitious of horses that have killed a fellow man.

That Peep not only had ridden the animal without help, but had broken its spirit completely, won its confidence, and led it back to the ranch was little short of unbelievable. Yet the T-7 hands voiced no wonder. They put it down simply as another feather in the bonnet of the steady-eyed, taciturn Peep, who long since had won acclaim as the most recklessly courageous rider on the Satanka range. Nor did they voice the added respect they felt. Cowland has little time for backslapping. The incident was quickly forgotten. It was just a more spectacular episode in the deadly routine they faced each day in their world of thundering hoofs.

Early August burned itself to a crisp beneath a blasting sun. The prairie carpet, splotched with patches of green, turned buff and seared and brown. Day after day the merciless sun crawled lazily through the heavens that hung above like a sea of glittering tin; each day the same, sickening and wilting. The few creeks that twisted across the arid flats became fetid, green-scummed pools. Hot winds whined constantly in the coulees, completing the destruction of the relentless sun. The Satanka range became an inferno of heat and tormenting insects—a land bereft of beauty, bone dry, blistered, panting.

But apparently the punchers paid no heed to the enervating weather, the mercury that climbed to fever heat during the day and dropped unbelievably during the night. From early dawn until after dark the hard-packed 'dobe yard of the T-7 resounded with the clatter of thundering hoofs; punchers coming and going, now gathering wild horses for the cavvy strings, now bringing the "salty" brutes in on a dead gallop to be thrown into round corrals. For the fall beef round-up was at hand. And beef round-up meant an insatiable demand for fresh horses that would stand up under the killing grind.

Bronc-peelers—flint eyed, bow-legged men, without fear of man or beast, paid by the head—turned the animals into cavvy mounts in short order—ridable but far from tractable. Many of the brutes were spoiled for life by inhuman treatment—a thing that Peep would not countenance when he personally had time to supervise the breaking out.

Each day found the big ranch in a bedlam. Sweating bronc-peelers tromped wicked outlaws in the three round corrals; shouts, curses, yells of derision arose in a crescendo of tumult. Horses pounded in and out; dust rolled in choking waves across the great fenced yard, beaten hard as concrete by hoofs and boots. Punchers ambled between the corrals and barns—a great chain of low-eaved log buildings. Others squatted in the shade mending saddles, braiding hondas, patching chaps and articles of clothing or bedrolls, stretching throw ropes. Night found the crew dog-tired and wilted by the sun, sprawled on their rolls in the two bunkhouses, content for the time being even to forego their penny ante for the blankets.

Thompson himself divided his time between the teeming wastes and the rambling two-story log ranchhouse—a landmark on the Satanka range. A structure huge and bulky was that T-7 ranchhouse—typical of those that once dotted rangeland but now are but shambled ruins in the ravages of time. Its massive side walls were of peeled cottonwood, bleached to a glaring white by summer sun and winter cold. Its gables were of rough pine siding that had known no paint, weather-beaten, stained with the dripping rains of forty years, the knots yellowed and still streaked with oozing pitch. The roof was straight-coned, steep-pitched, and covered with sun-curled shingles. In many places the pine boards had pulled away from the nails. On the front and side nearest the corrals was a porch that seemed to ramble round the structure and that at any time of day afforded some shade from the blazing sun.

At such times as he was in the ranch, Thompson was to be found on that porch, rocking violently in a creaky old chair. Old Jim seemed to find rest in that constant movement. And his dilapidated willow rocker was sedulously avoided when he was about.

A couple of evenings preceding the dawn on which the T-7 mess-wagon would rumble away on its great circle of cowland, Thompson galloped in on a lather-smeared and leg-weary horse. He had spent considerable time away from the ranch since Peep's encounter with Torpedo at the Ragged Hound corral, but so had many of the other punchers, and Thompson was never one to demand anything of his men he would not do himself.

But this night he was strangely preoccupied. His movements were abrupt and jerky, evidence of violent, stifled emotion. Swinging down at the barns and turning his half-dead horse over to a puncher, he motioned for Peep to follow and strode to the house. Wondering at the fact that the cowman, for all the sweat that streaked his grimy face and his attitude of abject weariness, did not throw himself sprawling into his favorite rocker on the porch, Peep went after him into the living-room, which also served as an office.

Once inside, he paused, his eyes surveying the room, while he waited for Thompson to speak. The gaunt cowman, obviously upset, started prowling about. Peep's gaze followed him strangely, to the end of the big room, with its massive native stone fireplace, its face blackened by years of roaring fires. The inevitable elk's head looked down from above the rough mantel, the prongs of its spiked horns cramped against the log beams that ran the length of the ceiling. The interior was murky in the shadows of evening, but two windows breaking the monotony of polished logs that rose to their sills. In the wan light the pictures that framed the 'dobe walls were vaguely discernible—the inevitable group picture of famous cattle shipments, a great calendar from a commission company, odds and ends of family ties done in chromo with gaudy frames. It was a typical western living-room with its horsehide furniture, battered and showing plainly the scratches of awkward, nervous rowels, a scarred desk in the corner piled high with dusty letters and papers.

"Somebody is swinging a long rope," Thompson announced abruptly after a time, halting spread-legged before Peep.

"Yeah?" If the young foreman was so much as surprised he gave no indication.

"Found six head of cows killed up yonder on Surprise Creek." The cowman went on with his nervous pacing. "They're not only swinging a long rope but they're using Winchesters to boot."

"Other spreads have been reporting losses for quite a spell," was Peep's drab rejoinder.

"But this is the first time they've hit us," Thompson boomed. "The critters were fresh T-7's."

"See anything of the calves?"

"Nothing but a warm trail."

"Heading which way?"

"North across the Flying Spear!"

"North across the Flying Spear?" In spite of his notorious calm, Peep started. The rustled calves were being moved across the Flying Spear, across his own ranch. "I was over every foot of that country today and never saw a rider," he said quickly. "Yet you say that calf trail was—"

"What were you doing on Surprise Creek?" Thompson demanded, noticeable suspicion in his voice.

"Nothing particular. Just riding."

"I ain't suspecting anybody." Thompson faced him, his great voice husky with suppressed rage. "But I'm repeating—somebody is swinging a long rope on my critters. They're trailing them across Flying Spear ground. They can rustle from the other outfits here on the Satanka all they want to. I don't care a damn how many the other spreads lose. But I can't afford to part with a single hoof."

He fell back to his nervous pacing. "I'm not sitting as pretty as most people think. The commission houses are crowding the T-7 hard. I—" He caught himself up, spun about. "It has got to stop, that's all."

It was Peep's first intimation that Thompson, the biggest taxpayer and easily the largest herdsman in the county, whose fenced pastures ran high into the thousands of acres, was not sound financially. Yet why the theft of six calves should arouse him to such a pitch as now evidently possessed him was beyond Peep's ken. While the cowman's discovery that stolen stuff was being trailed across the Flying Spear filled him with a vague uneasiness, it also angered him in a cold, unreasonable way, which, while he gave no outward indication of it, set him to smoldering inside.

He was positive that his father, before his recent death, had known nothing of any rustling. But as he tumbled the thing over in his mind he was not so positive about Tommy. He recalled that his brother had been singularly nervous when old Hank had bequeathed him the hair rope. The marked hair rope with the streak of yellow in it—and cautioned him against using it on any cattle but his own.

He jerked himself from his unpleasant thoughts, strode to a window to stare outside into the purple shadows that lay long over the greasewood and sage.

"Reckon the thing to do is to arm the hands," he offered quietly. "Let's boost their pay five bucks and slip out the order to shoot."

"That's just what I'm figuring on," Thompson said. "We haven't had rustlers working in T-7 stuff for years. Now that they have showed up, we can't let 'em get to breeding. They're just like flies when it comes to— They've monkeyed with the wrong walloper when they go to swinging their long ropes on my stuff. Line the boys up. Heel 'em for bear. Keep your eyes peeled. Sleep with one eye open. Find out if you can how come this stuff is being trailed across the Flying Spear. I'll keep a dally on my tongue about that angle until we know for dead certain what we're talking about. If it was to leak out right now you might have a hell of a hard time explaining."

Still Peep gave no outward sign of the seething within him. He faced big Jim and captured his roving gaze. Clockticks passed. The pantomime continued, each seemingly trying to pierce the veil of steely eyes and read behind.

"You're plumb right, Jim," Peep said evenly after a time. "And I'm much obliged to you for keeping quiet until we ferret things out."

Without another word he spun about and left the room, the big rancher, head down, starting anew his nervous pacing.

That night Peep lay awake turning the thing over in his mind. There seemed but one conclusion to draw. The fact that the stolen calves were moving across the Flying Spear—the little spread that Hank O'Day had left to him and Tommy—somehow seemed to implicate Tommy with the rustlers. A bitter thought for loyal Peep, but one which persisted in tormenting him for all he could do to drive it from his mind. He recalled Tommy's movements for weeks. Yet those movements appeared to exonerate him completely. And besides, he argued with himself, how could Tommy have any connection with a gang of rustlers —and he was satisfied that there was a gang if they had had the courage to start working in T-7 herds—and still have been with Thompson, old Hank, or himself almost constantly.

"The kid might be o'nery and reckless and hotheaded," he reasoned, "but I never heard of him stealing anything."

Having, to some extent, succeeded in convincing himself that Tommy knew no more of the thievery than he did, he fell into a fitful sleep. But a whistling hair rope with a streak of yellow braided into its strands, disturbed his chaotic dreams.

Chapter Four

HEELED HEAVY

DAWN BURST IN A FLING OF VIVID COLOR over the rim of the prairies. First a drab gray creeping into the greasewood to set it looming like misshapen creatures of a nightmare. Then, quickly, a shifting kaleidoscope of color—red, pink, orange. A flame—a burst of fire yellow—the tip of an infant sun popped into a sky that became brassy and metallic— a breathless, sickening calm that gave promise of another day of blistering heat.

Long before the crack of dawn Peep was up and about. The moon still hung like a great silver plaque in the ebon western sky when he pulled on his dew-damp boots and stepped from the bunkhouse into the chill morning air. Routing out the sleepy punchers, who awoke growling and cursing, he went on to the corrals, where, since the eventful day on Ragged Hound, he had kept Torpedo. The brute had been his one diversion, the single break in the deadly drab routine of ranch work and preparations for the round-up. A lover of fine animals, Peep had taken especial delight in winning the confidence of the outlaw. Torpedo had balked at the barn. In this one instance Peep had humored him. Somehow the youth seemed to understand the brute's aversion to confinement and cover when a prairie moon—that stirred some wild longing within himself—drenched the flats with a silver sheen.

"I like him because he's a natural born fighter," he had told the wondering punchers in reply to their puzzled questions and open warning that some day the outlaw would turn upon him and kill him.

They made no comment. Knowing Peep, the fighter,

they understood the bond that had arisen. Two natural-born fighters were bound to find some common ground even though one was a horse and the other a man.

Torpedo threw up his head at the approach of the young foreman. A snort whistled through his flaring nostrils. His long tail—untrimmed yet because of deadly hoofs—came up to bow like a weeping-willow limb. He trotted away, looking back, his movements tuned to mechanical perfection. It was that movement of the brute that fascinated Peep. The sorrel seemed to float over the ground. His hoofs possessed a rubber springiness that bounced him along at an amazing ease, a springiness that somehow suggested the smooth bounding of a running deer.

After he had circled the corral a couple of times, Torpedo slid to a halt and whirled. A flash of hatred flared into his eyes as Peep crawled through the poles. One ear plastered itself against his head, the other pricked forward inquisitively. His upper lip curled back to bare his teeth like a snarling dog. Peep spoke quietly, persuasively. The brute's rage vanished instantly. The fire left its eyes. The curl left its lips. The youth stood watching the outlaw for a moment, eyeing the plastered ear that flipped up and back, as though ashamed of the display of anger against that soothing voice, which Torpedo—in spite of his wild instinct—was learning to love and trust.

Making no attempt to touch the wary animal, Peep climbed back through the poles and went to the house. Despite the grumbling of the cook—shambling about the kitchen—he wheedled a handful of sugar. Then he went back to the corral.

Again he crawled through the corral poles, this time with his hand outstretched. Torpedo snorted savagely, dared a look, whirled and came forward cautiously, one ear still hesitant to join its forward fellow in an attitude of pleasure. When the brute had advanced far enough, it began stretching its long trim neck. Finally its tongue moved forth, succeeded in lapping a taste of sugar from the outstretched hand. Teeth clicked hungrily. Gone in a flash was Torpedo's fear. Both ears cocked forward with anticipation. He licked the hand clean of its offering of sweets.

"That's pretty larrupin' stuff, ain't it, pardner." Peep grinned, as the sugar overcame the sorrel's mistrust entirely. "Nobody ever bothered about feeding you sugar before, did they? Reckon that's why we are going to be real friends." He reached out to stroke the arched neck. But having decided suddenly that licking the outstretched hand was producing no more delectable sugar, Torpedo turned and walked disgustedly to the other side of the corral.

Peep followed leisurely. After several seconds of coaxing, he succeeded in getting to the brute's head, back against which that one ear again had plastered itself mistrustingly. With slow and cautious movements he scratched the ears beneath the halter the outlaw wore, raked his fingers along the worn hair beneath the cheek straps. Torpedo muzzled forward gingerly, twisted his head to and fro for the pleasant scratching. Then, almost before the brute realized it, Peep had swung onto its bare back, was lying along it, still scratching the ears.

Loath to leave off the pleasant rubbing, Torpedo jerked up his head. A snort whistled through his flaring nostrils. The plastered ear caught soothing words. But to no avail. The outlaw spirit burned within him. His head shot down to thread between taut, braced fetlocks. A slash of a quirt across a still sore shoulder brought it up, craning to see the manner of this thing who dared encroach upon that back without fear and speak into the plastered ear.

Violent trembling seized the outlaw. That quirt—the recollection of the terrific battle in the round corral on

Surprise Creek, the muscles that still ached and were sore—were all too vivid. Instinct warned Torpedo to be wary. This human had shown him nothing but kindness save the time that they had fought it out. But that was before they had come to an understanding.

Before he realized it, Torpedo had made a couple of short, wiry jumps. The quirt burned twice across his shoulder. He came up taut, began backing around the corral, shaking his head savagely.

"Reckon we understand each other right now," Peep whispered into the twitching ear. "Only you're supposed to go ahead instead of back. But that'll come in another lesson." He slid to the ground to resume scratching the ears. Once again Torpedo muzzled forward. "You'll be the top saddler in my string before you know it, you devil," Peep said, "and you're going on the round-up for all their fool warnings. I'm betting the ace on you, horse."

When the grumbling, swearing, shouts and raillery, the rattle of spur rowels, tinkle of milk pails, and whinnies of excited horses assured him that the punchers were all up and about, and the chore work well under way, Peep quit the corral. Torpedo followed him to the gate to stare after him.

"Come and get it, you coyotes, or I'll throw it out!" The cook's stentorian challenge to the hungry, waiting horde greeted him on the way to the house.

The laughter of the punchers, crowding about for a turn at the tin wash basin, and the sloshing of water ceased. They were trooping inside, fighting for position, when Peep came up. Their hearty greetings were evidence of the high regard in which they held the young foreman.

When they had arranged themselves at the long, oil-cloth-covered table with its inevitable pitcher of "golden drip" syrup, dish of stewed raisins and apples, and spoons sticking upright from a bowl in the center, he addressed them.

"Have you boys seen anything suspicious of late?" he asked quietly.

A series of surprised "no's" met the question. "Why?"

"Fresh T-7 cows with suckling calves are disappearing." Peep's announcement burst like a bombshell on the group and silenced them completely. "Somebody is using a Winchester on the cows, a long rope and a hot iron on the calves."

"Rustlers!" The word ran in an excited buzz around the table.

"You've guessed it," Peep remarked dryly. "And you can make up your mind they're hell-benders when they go to using rifles. Starting this morning, there are five bucks extra in your pay check. That's for oil for your Colts. Keep your eyes peeled and your guns unlimbered. Reckon while we're on beef round-up if we'll take a *pasear* up through those wild brakes on the upper Belle Fourche we'd find a likely place to do some tall nosing around. And remember, we're all riding this round-up heeled heavy."

"Ain't it about time you began packing your iron again?" one of the group demanded of Peep.

The young foreman swept the faces about him. Then he shoved the nose of a holstered forty-one to the table's rim. "I'm toting iron from now on," he said shortly. "Heeled heavy and fighting an itching trigger finger. Noticed any strangers around anywhere of late?"

"Why, yes," volunteered one of the punchers. "I saw a heavy-set, stocky-built walloper with a homely mug out yonder on the flats chewing the rag with Tommy the other day. He's a plumb stranger to these parts as far as I can recollect. I didn't ride too close, nor stop, so I didn't get a knockdown to the gent or get to learn what iron he's toting."

Peep felt his nerves go taut. He steeled himself against the new suspicion that suddenly flared up to torment him.

"Meet every stranger after this even if you have to ride out of your way to do it," he rasped out, twisting the holstered forty-one to a more comfortable position at his hip. "Starting today the season opens on long-rope swingers and cow-killing riflemen on the T-7 range." He picked up his fork and speared a piece of bacon as it came around. "And there is just plenty more coyote bounty where this first pay-raise comes from. Beef round-up starts in the morning. And we've got to locate something on it besides critters. Do you understand?"

The chorus of affirmative grunts assured him that they did.

"All right, then, when we swing out with dawn, we're not only riding for four-legged strays, but—" He left the sentence unfinished as he fell to eating moodily.

Chapter Five

An Old T-7 Custom

A FULL MOON HUNG LIKE A LANTERN in the western sky to drench the flats with a silver haze when the T-7 punchers rolled out, pulled on dew-damp boots, and stamped grumbling toward the barns. They were joined by other punchers, who crawled sleepily from tarps scattered about the big yard—"Reps" from neighboring outfits, who had come in during the night with their soogans and salty strings to ride with the T-7 beef pool, the biggest on the Satanka.

The corrals were choked with wild-eyed, snorting horses that milled and whinnied, kicked and squealed with savage glee. Up from the home pasture came the wrangler, driving before him a thundering, playful remuda. The big place became a bedlam of confusion, shouts, bawls, curses, laughter that rose in a crescendo.

Before the crack of dawn the crew had breakfasted. Tarps were rolled, piled high onto the bed-wagon, and lashed to the standards. Shying, kicking string horses were roped out, dragged forth, and saddled. The pilot for the day cursed and fumed at the delay, strove to quiet his frightened bronc, which fought the bit until his mouth dripped bloody foam as it curveted and backed around in the milling mass.

At a word from Peep—who seemed everywhere at once, with his customary thoroughness overlooking not one single detail—sets of four salty broncs were coaxed and cursed into the traces of the bed-wagon and the mess-wagon. The snarling cook climbed onto the first, gathered up the reins of the lunging, wild-eyed brutes the puncher held with difficulty. The nighthawk scrambled to a perilous perch on the bedrolls, wedged himself in where he could foot the brake.

"Let 'er go!" The eight broncs were released with slaps across the rumps and shouts. The traces snapped taut. The heavy wagons lurched ahead, careened away to the accompaniment of yells of derision, the rattle and bang of pots and pans that goaded the green broncs to a frenzy. Once the cook and nighthawk had managed to steer the tough-mouthed brutes—running with the bits between clenched teeth—through the gate, they shook out the reins. With the pilot in the lead, the wagons went lurching dangerously across the brush and coulees up Surprise Creek in the general direction of the designated noon camp.

The racing remuda got away ahead of a yipping wrangler. In the lead ran Torpedo, bucking with the sheer joy of freedom, squealing gleefully, kicking and shying at imaginary terrors lurking in the brush. The wrangler had wailed loudly and long at having to take the brute along. But Peep was adamant, refused stubbornly to be parted from the horse even for the duration of the round-up. An open protest to Jim Thompson had brought no results. Jim seldom interfered where his foreman was concerned. Peep O'Day had been wagon-boss of the T-7 pools since he was a youngster. And not even big Jim questioned his supremacy in that position. He paid Peep to handle his spread, paid the youth top wages for his seemingly limitless knowledge of cattle. And Jim knew what everyone else knew, that Peep O'Day, through tireless work and conscientious service, had built the T-7 into the biggest spread on the Satanka.

At a word from Peep the punchers took to their saddles. Hell suddenly broke loose. The air was filled with whoops and yowls, the fiendish squeals of ponies which, with humps in their backs, pitched away toward the gate. Punchers went skyward to the howling delight of their companions. Riderless ponies started to run with empty stirrups flapping, only to be set back on their haunches or "busted" by ready and whining ropes and re-mounted, this time to be "tromped down" by a cursing, dirt-covered, and shame-faced buckaroo.

Presently the churning mass had taken some sort of definite form, with every man in the saddle. It straightened out, was gone in a choking cloud of dust. The big T-7 beef pool was on its way!

After the cowboys had swung off up Surprise Creek, Peep lingered on at the corral. But there was nothing of the stern-faced wagon-boss about the worried youth that morning, nothing of the man who snapped orders at a tough lot and got immediate results. He was plainly nervous, ill at ease. And, although he made a show of working, he kept one eye cocked anxiously on the house.

Presently he heard the door open. He busied himself with his throw rope and a last minute inspection of his latigo. Footsteps came nearer. He looked up to face Tommy.

"Thought you had gone on with the crew," the brother remarked carelessly.

"I hung back on purpose," Peep said. "I wanted to have a little talk with you."

"Preaching again?" Tommy's tone was ugly.

"No." Peep's face tightened. "But Jim was telling me—" He caught himself up quickly on the point of revealing the facts of the rustling, the apparent implication of the Flying Spear, as Thompson had told him. "There are rustlers at work on the Satanka."

"There are rustlers in every cow country, aren't there?" Tommy snorted, leading his mount from the corral and for all its shying and lunging, tossing a saddle on it.

"But—" Peep plainly was at a loss how to voice the thing in his mind. "I understand from the boys that you were seen talking to a stranger out on the flats the other day."

"So that's it?" Tommy sneered. "Because I talked to a stranger, you figure—"

"I'm not figuring anything," Peep cut him short. "I was wondering who that stranger was?"

"I don't know myself." Tommy savagely kicked the wind from his mount's swollen belly and jerked the latigo to the last notch. "Just some jasper I rode onto. Not a bad sort of fellow—said he was riding through—some drifter. . . ."

"I'd be a little careful, Tommy," Peep cautioned. "Something has come up—I'm not at liberty to say right now—but it affects you and me pretty closely. After this, if you meet any strangers, find out—"

"Yeah." Tommy swung into the saddle. "I'll get his picture and his pedigree for you." He lifted his horse in a gumbo-flinging lunge and, without looking back, raced after the wagons, now but a spiral of dust swirling along toward Ragged Hound.

Peep hung onto his mounting anger with an effort. It had always been thus with him and Tommy: he trying to play the part of a father since the death of old Hank, Tommy resentful, deliberately attempting to hurt him, ignoring his advice.

"Damn him," he growled. "I wish I hadn't planned to take him along with the wagon. He's worthless on the round-up. He won't work, and I'm leery. But why the devil should I always be fretting myself about him."

Unconsciously he had voiced the question that had been uppermost in his mind for weeks. Why should he concern himself about Tommy, who had always had the best of everything? Since childhood Tommy had been closest to the heart of old Hank, who, in spite of Peep's constant warnings that some day he would regret not having curbed the youth, only had made a greater effort to grant his every wish. Old Hank had openly boasted of Tommy's exploits and popularity, to which the reticent Peep did not aspire. Many times when Tommy had shifted the blame for some wild escapade, Peep had endured it in silence for their father's sake, stifling his rage with the thought that, after all, Tommy was young, and his brother. But now, for all he could do, Peep realized that they were drifting to a showdown that presently would burst about them.

Yet, strangely, for all their constant bickering, only once before old Hank's death had they come near a serious break. That was when they had both fallen in love with Hope Thompson, the adopted daughter of big Jim.

A trim little thing was Hope, the only child of home-steaders, orphaned when a fire had swept their patented section and seething flames had claimed her parents. There were few neighbors on the Big Satanka range, and fewer women. And because she had nowhere else to go— this little morsel of humanity, who even as a child had gorgeous hair shot with gold, wide, pleading blue eyes and features that were cameos of clearness—Thompson had taken her to the T-7. There he employed a nursemaid for the youngster. She blossomed like a gumbo lily, became the beauty of the range. Every man in cowland was secretly in love with her. But none dared profess the love their eyes could not conceal. For she was one of them, a tomboy raised to ride and shoot and rope with the best of the lot. She was a pal to everybody, and as such commanded a respect that was almost religious.

Then, almost on an instant, Tommy and Peep had fallen prey to her charms. Big Jim had quickly solved the problem and averted trouble between the two by bundling Hope up and sending her off to boarding-school in the East. Within six months Tommy had forgotten her completely. But Peep was not the kind to forget. He still cherished the girlish image of Hope in his heart. And now—

Hope had come back to the T-7 the night before. Her

arrival had been unexpected. He had gotten the news from one of the punchers, who had chanced to be in Satanka and had brought her out late. As a rule, Hope's periodic home-comings were eventful and marked with elaborate celebrations. But this time she had come unannounced. Peep had been too dead tired even to hear them when they arrived; only by chance had he learned that morning that she was there. In the rush of work in getting the round-up started he had found no time to offer even a word of welcome. So he lingered on, hoping that she might— Had he been Tommy, he would have gone to the house. But for all his reckless, dashing courage, Peep O'Day was shy as a chipmunk around women. He could only hope, and curse savagely because Tommy had the temerity to go to the house before he pulled out and bid good-by.

"Good morning—and good-by!" a low husky voice at his elbow brought Peep whirling about. Before him stood Hope. But a different Hope than he had known, a girl blossomed into gorgeous womanhood, with charming poise and confidence.

He blinked and gulped; the things he had many times thought of saying fled. This girl was no longer the Hope of their childhood days, of overalls and fancy stitched boots. For she wore a tailored riding-habit and highly polished boots, which made her look even younger and lovelier. Her eyes were just the same, large, frank, a deep lake-blue. Her skin was just as smooth and tanned, glowing with healthy color. The same gold shot the fine-spun hair that strayed about her face in the droning breeze.

Peep was conscious of all this in a single glance. Yet for the life of him, now that he had the opportunity, he could think of nothing to say. His own strained thoughts made conversation difficult. But only for a moment.

"I see you're waiting for me." She smiled, a contagious smile that lighted her whole face, made her eyes twinkle

and revealed beautiful pearly teeth.

"Well—there was just a few things to tend to before—" He groped about for words. "It's a big pool this year and the detail—" He was nervously aware that again his eyes were devouring the trim figure before him.

"You haven't forgotten there's an old custom around the T-7—a custom that dates back—oh, ever so long."

He smiled. "What was it we used to call it?" he said soberly. "It's been so long. . . . Oh, yes, 'bidding the wagon-boss good-by.' "

"Well," pettishly, "is my horse ready, wagon-boss?"

Gone in a flash was his reserve. For all her modish attire, it was the same Hope—Hope of the childhood days, bubbling over with health and sheer love of living.

"Well," he confessed sheepishly. "Your horse is—"

She laid a hand on his arm. A simple, friendly gesture yet it set him to tingling. "Then you hadn't forgotten?"

"Forgotten?" He whipped her an amazed glance. "I took a chance that mebbeso—"

"You knew I'd come," she said shortly. "Lead forth the mount, sire, the lady would fain ride a piece to the round-up with the wagon-boss." She spun about and ran to the barn. He dashed after her to enter and reappear shortly leading her horse, already saddled. He helped her up, swung into his own saddle, and they headed toward the gate.

"Let's see, how many round-ups have we—" he began.

"Have I, you mean," she bantered. "What you're trying to ask is how many pool round-ups have I ridden a way with the wagon-boss?" Her brows puckered thoughtfully. "Let's see—I'm going on twenty—you are twenty-two. You started wrangling for Jim when you were twelve. Do you remember that first round-up?" She threw back her head and went into peals of laughter. "You didn't have a saddle. Uncle Hank was afraid you'd get dragged in a stirrup. You were a determined little cuss—you wrangled that year with a gunnysack for a saddle."

Her mood was contagious. He too fell to laughing.

Suddenly she grew serious, "Peep," she said, as they rode knee to knee through the hush of dawn, "I notice—you're wearing your gun again. Have you forgotten?"

"No," he said quietly. "I've kept my word, Hope, until today. For five years I haven't toted a gun. But—Jim found evidence of rustlers yesterday. I didn't buckle this on just because— It's business; this round-up has a lot ahead of it. I'm sorry if—"

"Never mind, Peep," she said soberly. "I—I guess I understand. Although I've gotten some strange ideas of things, back East. But if Jim told you to wear your gun—Are the others—do you all have guns on this pool?"

"Yes. And we're on fighting-pay."

His abrupt answer made her gasp.

"I don't like it," she flashed. "And I'm going to tell Jim so as quickly as I get back. All the cows on earth aren't worth one of you boys—to me. And Peep, another thing—they tell me you've taken Torpedo along in your string."

"Best horse on the Satanka," he boasted. "Why, Hope, you'll be riding that sorrel before long. He's a dream."

"A nightmare to me." She shuddered. "But I know anything I can say will have no effect on changing your mind. But I do wish you'd be careful."

He laughed at her seriousness. "The East has got you, hasn't it, Hope," he said smilingly. "You've been away from this rough and tumble existence so long, I don't wonder at it. But don't you worry that pret—that head of yours a minute. Torpedo and I are pals. And," he stroked the holstered gun caressingly, "this gun never comes out of that holster unless—unless—"

"I hope it never comes for any reason, Peep."

He stared straight ahead into the lifting dawn, a soft light that was bringing the sagebrush and greasewood into silhouette. A meadowlark teetered in the top of a sage and warbled gaily. A coyote sprang up before them, started slinking through the brush. Quicker than a flash, Peep's gun had leaped to the rim of its holster. A streak of orange powder-flame laced the dawn. The coyote bounded into the air, kicked convulsively, and straightened out. Peep broke the gun, blew through the barrel, and rammed it back into the holster. He turned to the girl with a smile. But that smile froze on his lips. She was staring at him hard, searching his face with a look that was almost terror.

"Why, Hope," he gulped. "What—what—"

She drew rein. "Peep," she cried. "To be able to shoot like that is— It's a curse. A curse, I tell you. I wish you'd never seen a gun, Peep; it frightens me to see that holster on you again. If you only—" She caught herself up sharply. "I've ridden far enough," she said soberly. "Jim will be 'a-faunchin' if I don't get back." She offered her hand. He took it gingerly.

"So-long, Hope," he said.

"So-long, Peep. And please—remember your promise about that gun."

Before he could answer she had whirled her pony, lifted it with the rowels, and was gone, waving back to him over her shoulder.

Chapter Six

Torpedo Breaks Through

THE DAYS THAT FOLLOWED were busy ones for the T-7 pool riders, and especially for Peep, who expected no more from his men than he was willing to do himself. At best a round-up is a killing grind; a grind that breaks strong men down; frays their nerves and stiffens their joints; a deadly grind that crushes the spirit from horses and reduces them to leg-weary automatons.

The daily routine of the big T-7 pool was no different from that of any other round-up. Before dawn the nighthawk thundered in with his cavvy. The brutes were run into a rope corral—a V-shaped enclosure formed by stringing ropes from the front and back wheels of the wagons. Having corraled the remuda within the makeshift corral, the nighthawk gathered chips, built the fire, kicked the snoring cook in the ribs, and before "cookie" could heave a boot, or a can of beans, ducked into his bedroll for a wink of sleep.

Soon the savory odor of coffee and bacon set the punchers squirming in their soogans. But it took the cook's lusty bawl of, "Come and get it or we'll throw it out!" to bring them yawning and stretching from their bedrolls to tug on dew-damp boots, arm themselves with tin cup and plate, and drop cross-legged on the ground.

During the breakfast of "dough-gods," beans, bacon or steaks, cooked deliciously in a Dutch oven, Peep posted his circle riders, gave orders as to the territory they were to cover, and good-naturedly cussed the sleepy-eyed punchers into action. It was at breakfast that wagon-bosses were made or broken. And it was there that Peep O'Day won the devotion of his riders. For never once did he raise his voice, never did he threaten or browbeat. As a result, he got the maximum of work; T-7 pools moved swifter and covered greater areas than other round-up crews.

Breakfast over, Peep ordered two of the best ropers into the rope corrals with the wild-eyed, snorting remuda. Each puncher singled out his mount for the day. The ropers caught them. The brutes were dragged forth, fore-feet planted, backs humped, eyes skinned to the whites. Saddles were thrown aboard. One by one the punchers "stepped across," some to sit on curveting mounts and hurl jibes at others who went skyward on vicious snake-eyes to land in the saddle or root dirt with their noses.

Once the circle riders were mounted, they set forth in the cool dawn to ride the draws and hogbacks of a given territory, for, as Peep tried to explain to a dis-gusted Tommy around a campfire early in the round-up, cattle feed up the ravines in the daytime and return to water at night. But Tommy refused to listen, and brand-ing Peep's remarks as trash, strode off in high dudgeon.

The dishes washed, the wagons again were loaded and started for the noon camp, already designated by Peep. By the time the puncher's clock—the sun—registered mid-day, the circle riders had begun to straggle in with their pick-ups, which were thrown together to form the day herd.

Day after day the monotonous routine continued. But it was the evenings, when Peep found himself dog-tired and restless, that were most difficult. For then the hard part of range life begins. Selecting a bedground on high ground—floods were a constant menace in the fall of the year on the Satanka—where grass was good, Peep would ride onto a point while the day herders worked the graz-ing herd slowly toward him. Here the brutes were put into an easy mill—the leaders turned back and the drags pushed forward—until the herd was moving in an endless circle. If not crowded, the brutes would mingle and fall to feeding. Then the regular punchers, who had already eaten their supper, would relieve the day herders and "killpecker" guard was established to bed down the cattle.

The nights, too, were endless to Peep, for they set him to thinking—of Hope. The star-spangled sky filled him with a strange and restless emotion he was powerless to overcome. When the moon creeping over the rim of the prairie flooded the flats with its soft effulgent glow, the restlessness he could not explain lay heaviest on his soul. Then he would seek out Torpedo and work for hours with the outlaw—which now followed him with the blind devotion of a dog; or he would relieve his own herders to stand guard over the cattle. If the herders wondered, they said nothing. The hard-working, taciturn Peep O'Day was ever a mystery to the cowhands on the Satanka.

As the days passed, one thing struck Peep, ever alert to every sign of rangeland, as strange. The strays they picked up on circle were bunched, and showed a surprising lack of fear of horses. To Peep this meant two things: either it was sign of an early winter, the herds instinctively moving into the sheltered country, or the strays were familiar with riders and had been bunched recently. The latter conclusion pointed to rustlers working ahead of the round-up.

Rustlers! The word was a by-word in the camp. Talk around the fire at nights invariably turned to rustlers. Conjectures, imaginings, weirdly elaborated tales. But never during the days was a strange rider sighted. If there were losses, the rustlers had chosen to lie low while the armed riders were abroad and bide their time for the pick-ups.

Due to the bunching of the strays, Peep was forced on the third day to order the day herd worked because it had grown too unwieldy to handle. On a greasewood flat above the roily Belle Fourche, the punchers, thankful for a respite in the monotonous circle riding, set to work.

But an incident in the morning somewhat relieved the monotony. Peep that day had ridden Torpedo. The men had watched him rope the brute in the round corrals— he would allow no one else to do the roping. He had not dragged the animal forth as had the others. He had coaxed and petted it outside until Torpedo was trailing along behind him like a work horse anticipating its grain. Once outside, he had saddled the outlaw with little difficulty. As the latigo drew tight, Torpedo had given vent to snorting, explosive rage. The punchers, who had ceased their work to watch, fell to wagering. But it was Tommy, ever sullen now with weariness, who brought the climax.

"Ten to one he don't ride him slick!"

Peep whirled at the sound of his brother's voice. His face went pale, deathly pale. The punchers backed away, for there was tension in the air as the brothers faced each other. Clock-ticks passed, deadly, ominous, pregnant with the possibilities for a showdown. Then somewhere a steer bawled. The tension snapped. Tommy slunk back, but the scornful voice of Peep followed him.

"I'll go you one better." Peep's tone was stinging as a whip-lash. "I'll make it a hundred to one you haven't got the guts even to climb aboard him."

The punchers waited for Tommy to accept the challenge. He never opened his mouth. A loud guffaw went up. But Peep was by no means finished.

"I'm calling that ten to one I don't ride him, Tommy," Peep fired on at the callow youth. "Calling you for exactly the amount you make on this round-up at the rate of one to ten I do ride him slick. And a hundred to one you haven't got the guts to get onto him."

There passed another moment of silence. But Tommy had thrown himself onto a horse and was roweling away from the camp.

Quietly Peep stepped across Torpedo. Only once did the outlaw so much as shy. That was when Peep, having ridden him up alongside the bed-wagon, lifted an arm to direct his men. Torpedo threaded his nose between his fetlocks, made one half-hearted lunge. A slash of the quirt across his shoulder brought that head up. The brute trotted off amid the cheers of the punchers.

Later that day the punchers worked the day herd. Beneath a brassy sun, foam-splattered ponies darted out of the restless sea of cattle with dodging steers which were run into smaller bunches guarded by punchers holding the cut.

Cows with calves hugging their flanks lumbered from the herd, wicked-eyed little cutting-horses pounding at their heels and nipping their rumps. Lariats whined. Calves tumbled in fighting, bawling heaps. Calf wrestlers, covered with blood and perspiration, were upon them instantly, pinioning their flailing legs. From a chip fire came hot irons in the hands of soot-blackened cowboys. Terrified bleats, the sizzle of seared flesh, the pungent odor of burning hair and the animals scrambled to their feet and raced back to frantic mothers, licking the fresh brands as they ran.

Beside the fire stood two burly notchers, dripping knives in their hands. As the brute went down for the iron, those knives fell to notch an ear or a dewlap.

The scene was one of utter confusion. The shouts and curses of the cowboys mingled with the bawling of steers, the lowing of cows, and the bleats of calves to produce a deafening tumult.

Then of a sudden, above the bedlam, arose a hoarse bawl which brought the men straight in their saddles. There was no mistaking it. The challenge of a steer suddenly gone on the prod.

The cattle lunged away from a big, raw-boned critter which, with head lowered and tail straight out behind, charged down on Tommy O'Day. Cornered, Tommy swept the heaving wall of flesh about him with a wild glance, gave his pony rein, and drove home the rowels.

The horse reared with a violent, twisting motion, wheeled on its hind legs, and lunged from the path of the locoed steer. Blinded with fury, the brute came on, sending the terrified cattle up on one another's backs in frantic efforts to stay clear of it. From every side cowboys were fighting to open a lane to the scene of combat.

Peep's voice cracked out above the bedlam like a whiplash. "Dodge him! If you can get to your rope, bust him. But for God's sake, don't shoot. Spilling blood will stampede the herd."

Tommy heard the order even above the uproar. But hemmed in by cattle far more fearful of the slavering steer than of his pony, dodging the brute for any length of time was impossible. Roping him in the tight-packed mass was entirely out of the question. The one hope he could see was to break through the herd, but in trying to reach him the punchers themselves were wedging the frightened animals closer about him.

He drove his pony deeper among the jostling animals, trusting to its agility and instinct to stay clear of the maddened brute until help came. Suddenly the horse slipped on a stretch of wet earth and went down. It bumped along on its knees, trying to regain its feet. Before it could rise, the steer was upon it. With a terrific sweep of its horns it laid open the pony's shoulder.

Tommy threw himself from the saddle, missed a footing, and sprawled headlong in the choking mass. Above the sluicing roar of his own hot blood in his ears he heard the swish of the brute's horns and felt the rush of air as they grazed his back. Clawing dirt from his eyes, he scrambled to his feet. One glimpse of the wounded pony, struggling to rise, and terror took possession of him, stark, frantic terror that halted his faculties. He clawed frantically for his Colt. Now the steer was just above him, a huge, gigantic object ready to tear the life from him. He jerked up his gun.

"Don't shoot! It will stampede the herd. They'll tromp you to death!" It was Peep's voice. *Cool,* Tommy thought. *Damnably cool!* How could Peep be so cool when—

To hell with the herd. That steer!

"Get a horse in there—" Peep's voice came from far, far away.

"There ain't a horse that'll go through!" The bawl of a puncher rang like a tocsin in Tommy's ears.

Not a horse that would come through the frenzied mass to him. He was trapped—he would be gored— Again the gun came up.

"The hell there ain't a horse will go through! Get back! Give me room!" It was Peep's voice cracking, sharp. "Watch this Torpedo go through! Don't shoot, Tommy. I'm coming. For God's sake, hang on!"

Came a mighty thunder of hoofs. Tommy was only half conscious of the fact that cattle were bounding away from him on every side. He raised his gun, fired wildly into space. Just then something happened. A great shapeless mass was plunging toward him. He saw it but vaguely. Then a horse was towering over him, bowling cattle aside like tenpins. He caught the color. Sorrel—a slash face— his head was up, nostrils flaring. It was plunging, madly, frantically, by sheer brawn and nerve tromping down anything that dared resist its advances.

Then suddenly he was alone—was on his knees, pumping lead into the ground. A weird cry roused him. Torpedo stood just above—Torpedo, pawing the ground with impatience—Torpedo whinnying a savage challenge at cattle bolting in every direction.

A strong arm encircled him. He was jerked off the ground, lifted high in the air. Then blackness closed over him.

Tommy struggled back to consciousness. His first thought was of voices above him. He felt hot and cold, nerveless, spineless. Then he pried his eyes open—Peep was bending above him—

Came to him the words of a cowboy, almost reverently: "Damn me, I'll take back everything I've ever said about that Torpedo horse. He's the first brute I ever saw with guts enough to tackle a crazy day herd. He's a prize, Peep. If it hadn't been for Torpedo, Tommy would have—"

Tommy gazed up into Peep's anxious eyes.

"All right, kid?" came a hurried query.

"I reckon so." Some strange trait in Tommy brought the mean to the foreground. "But did I kill that damned steer? Did I stampede the herd?"

He thought he detected just a smile on Peep's lips. "Stampede nothing—you didn't even pull the trigger, you were so scared. It was Torpedo broke through, where all the other horses refused. Torpedo killed Paw, Tommy, but he saved your life."

"Damn Torpedo," Tommy snorted, getting to his feet to stand swaying dizzily. "And I wish I'd stampeded the whole T-7 herd. What do you think of that?"

Chapter Seven

TOMMY THIS AND TOMMY THAT

FALL SHIPPING WAS IN FULL SWING in the one-story cowtown of Satanka. Cowboys in unwieldy yellow oilskin slickers clumped about in the cold drizzle which, since dawn, had drenched the village to turn the narrow, rutty street into a slippery lane of sticky gumbo. The rickety boardwalks oozed water. Water dripped from the false fronts of the score of weather-beaten buildings, the dirty panes of which peered like sightless eyes through the afternoon gloom.

Ponies huddled at the hitch rails, weight on three legs, heads down, rumps to the storm beating in from the greasewood flats on a wind that whined and howled mournfully. But a mockery of civilization at the best, Satanka, slashed by rain, now presented a dismal picture, a picture of utter desolation.

In the stock pens below the storm-whipped railroad station, humped-back, shivering cattle bellowed. From the river bottoms, where other dripping herds were held for empty cars, came a medley of raucous bawls that seemed to echo the utter dreariness which gripped the region.

Citizens scooted to cover here and there, to stare out gloomily from the interior of stores, dark and uninviting in aspect. Saloons were crowded with hard-faced, unshaven punchers, who, after endless weeks on the silent trails, craved the entertainment that Satanka offered. Raw as it was, they were eager to spend the hard-earned, uneasy money that burned their pockets.

When the last T-7 critter had been loaded, Peep O'Day gave a few low-voiced orders to his men, dragged his great saddle slicker closer about him, climbed over the rail of the stockyards, and sloshed away through the ankle-deep ooze. Plowing across the railroad tracks, he headed toward town. Once on the dreary, rain-drenched street, he paused in the shelter of the false front of a building and fished in his pockets for "the makin's."

"Reckon I'd better be shagging right along for the T-7," he muttered aloud, twisting a cigaret and ducking low against the lashing rain to cup a match to the tip. "There will be plenty of work to be done now that the round-up is over. Hadn't ought to have let Tommy go on it, damn it. I suppose I'll have to round him up and—" He straightened up to inhale deeply and let the smoke drift from his nostrils. "He'll like as not get to raising hell with the punchers. And there's just plenty of tough wallopers here itching to raise hell." A couple of nervous drags and he snapped the cigaret savagely into a puddle of water in the street. While his father had been alive it had not seemed so bad, this constant consideration of Tommy. But now that old Hank was gone, he somehow rebelled at the idea.

Still he stood on in the shelter of the building, prey to riotous thoughts that took no notice of time. Now it was Hope as he had last seen her on Ragged Hound. Now Tommy—all his life it had been Tommy. Tommy this, Tommy that. And the role of guardian to the inconsiderate Tommy galled bitterly.

"I don't owe Tommy anything," he growled, whirling out from the protection of the building, and sloshing through the mud and water back toward the livery barn. "Let him take care of himself once and find out what it feels like."

A few paces and he stopped. As many times before in the past weeks his father's voice seemed to ring in his ears: "I'm—scared—for Tommy." The words came halting, breathless, the words of a dying man: "He's—hot—headed —reckless. You—are—his—keeper—Peep—like—the—Good Book—says. Swear—"

Spinning about, he retraced his steps, splashed across the muddy street up onto the sodden walk, and entered the Jumbo saloon, the favorite retreat of Satanka stockmen.

The place reeked with the smell of wet leather and stale beer. It was jammed with yelling punchers, men of the sagebrush, breeds, all sun-blackened, muddy, and thirsty. Tallow-kneed punchers lined the bar. Punchers with linked arms swayed to the ear-splitting discord of coyote falsetto and maudlin bass. Here and there a happy-go-lucky waddy danced through the crowd with a chair clasped affectionately in his arms.

The foul liquor of the Jumbo was getting in its work. The scene was riotous, boisterous, yet touched with a heart-rending poignancy of lonely men—men craving companionship—of women—good women.

Failing to locate Tommy at once in the milling crowd, Peep walked to the bar, where he leaned, idly surveying the scene. Culling the hard faces with eyes that were steel —poker tables with their torn coverings—dusty bottles on the back bar—tiers of delicate, yet murky glasses, seldom used to serve the uncouth patrons who demanded, "Somethin' solid as would serve to hold a he-man shot."

His glance roved on to the galaxy of beauties in tights which decorated the wall. Full-form portraits torn from the pages of a pink magazine and placed with the eye of a connoisseur of pretty women. He knew them by heart. Yet in spite of his abstraction he became conscious of something new in the collection. He moved close to read it:

$1,000 REWARD

Will be paid for information leading to the arrest and conviction of rustlers stealing from the T-7.

JIM THOMPSON, *Owner.*

Old Jim sure is going strong, Peep mused grimly. *If those long-rope swingers are tough I reckon Jim is doing some mighty poor advertising for himself and the T-7.*

"Have a drink?" A thick, husky voice at his elbow cut in on his thoughts.

Peep turned slowly. A heavy-set fellow, with little, beady black eyes and a piggish face almost the color of his water-logged leather chaps, was leering at him drunkenly.

"Thanks, I never use it," Peep answered.

"You're getting pretty cocky all of a sudden to refuse to drink with me!" the stranger blurted, thick-tongued.

Peep gauged him with a coldly glittering eye. His flashy apparel, shot with rosettes, which marked him as a new-comer to the Satanka range, accentuated the brutality of his face. Peep's gaze roved from the gun, belted high at his hip, upward along a fat, pock-marked face with purple pouches, finally to meet the unfriendly stare of little, watery eyes. For no reason at all he asked himself if this, by chance, could be the fellow the T-7 punchers had seen talking with Tommy, and if the man now had mistaken him for his brother.

"Take it any way you want to," Peep returned coldly after a time. "I don't drink with you or anyone else. Not because I'm against the stuff particularly for those who crave it, but I just don't like it and it doesn't set good with me." For the first time he now noticed that half a dozen other strangers had moved up suddenly and were watching them.

"No hombre ever I met up with can refuse to drink with me," the piggish-faced individual boasted. "And you're one in particular who can't. Have a ginger ale?"

"I said I didn't drink!" Peep flung back softly.

At that moment a group of new arrivals entered and elbowed between them. Taking violent hold on his mounting anger, and hating any kind of rowdyism, Peep started through the crowd. He found Tommy, presently, the center of a jovial group, his face flushed and his tongue thick from liquor.

"I'm heading for the T-7," Peep told him curtly. "You'd better come along."

"I've got a little business that needs attending to," Tommy replied carelessly.

Something in his brother's tone caused Peep to wonder what business was so important as to demand his attention so late that day. He edged closer and spoke in an undertone. "I wouldn't get salivated and go to gambling."

"Rattle your hocks and tend to your muleys," Tommy jeered. "Shag on back to the T-7. Get the milking done, and be sure you don't forget to bed down the horses."

A burst of maudlin laughter greeted the sally. Peep bit his lip, spun about, and with spur rowels raking the rough board floor, strode out of the saloon. On his way to the livery barn he unexpectedly encountered Jim Thompson.

"Where's Tommy?" the rancher asked, backing into the shelter of a building.

"Over at the Jumbo.".

"Hope came in to see the finish of the round-up."

Peep was conscious of his violent start. "Hope—"

"Unexpectedly—" Thompson was saying. "I suppose the kid does get lonesome, but this is no place for her. I wondered if Tommy wouldn't drive her home in my buckboard. I've made all plans to take a *pasear* up the river and see if I can't get a line on those long-rope swingers by working down slow and easy and talking to the other stockmen. I'd ask you to take her out, but I reckon you've got your hands full. You're more valuable if you shagged it down to the T-7 and looked after things instead of wasting time jogging along in the buckboard."

Peep scarcely heard old Jim to a finish. His heart was thumping too loudly against his ribs. Hope Thompson in Satanka! Hope alone—and the town swarming with drunken punchers,

"I reckon Tommy will be glad to take her out," he found himself muttering. "You might go over to the Jumbo and see before I hit the trail."

"Thanks!" Thompson swung on his heel. After he had disappeared into the saloon, Peep entered a drugstore and stood staring out at the dripping world. It was there Thompson found him sometime later.

"Tommy says he'll take her," the cowman announced. "If you've got everything wound up, you'd better shag along for the ranch now. You might keep your eye peeled for Hope. If she don't show up when you figure her and Tommy ought to, lope out a piece to meet 'em." His hand fell to the door knob. "By the way, Tommy's gambling a bit. Don't know who he's playing with, but he was betting, high, wide, and handsome, when I went into the Jumbo, There ain't nothing I can tell you that you don't know about the ranch. Look for me when you see me. So-long!"

"So-long, Jim!"

As Peep uttered the words he was conscious of a heavy feeling—a hollow, depressing sensation, as though he was bidding good-by to a friend forever. At a loss to explain it, he pulled himself together sharply only to be assailed by a new worry that drove all else from his mind.

It's a danged hard road to the T-7 when it's good, he mused, let alone when it's raining pitchforks and those gumbo flats are knee-deep in water. Some of those dry washes will be bank-full. The river crossing at the ranch will be a ticklish piece of fording. If Tommy isn't plumb sober he'll never make it out there with Hope. Reckon I'll just get them started before I pull out, then mosey along behind in case they need help.

Quitting the drugstore, he sloshed across the street, and again elbowed his way into the Jumbo.

Chapter Eight

THE SIX-GUN CURSE

JUST INSIDE THE SALOON, Peep halted. Throwing open his great slicker and flipping the water from it, he searched the milling crowd for Tommy. Presently, through the haze of cigaret smoke that eddied upward to drift in layers along the raftered ceiling, he located him, hunched over a poker table. Across from him sat the piggish-faced stranger. If Peep had disliked the fellow at their first meeting, his opinion was in nowise changed by this second look. And to find him now as Tommy's opponent not only angered him unreasonably but increased the suspicion— that for some unknown reason had taken firm hold of him —that this was the man whom the T-7 punchers had sighted on the range talking with his brother.

Tommy's voice, high-pitched, uncertain, arose above the bedlam. "And I'll just take a look at that pat hand of yours for a hundred bucks!"

Peep snapped straight. He elbowed his slicker aside. His thumbs dropped down to hook in his cartridge belt. In a half-dozen strides he was across the saloon, had stopped beside the pair.

"Hold on there," he rasped out at Tommy. "Where are you getting any hundred bucks to look at a pat hand with? Tell me that."

His brother stared up through eyes dulled with liquor, lurched to his feet.

"It's none of your damned business!" he blurted out thickly.

"The hell it ain't," Peep shot back. "If you're betting that money Paw left in the bank—"

"What if I am?" Tommy cut in to snarl savagely. "He

left half of it to me, didn't he? I don't have to ask you for a nickel every time I want one, do I?"

"Mebbe not," Peep conceded, "but you can't spend a cent of it until we go to the bank together and get it fixed up." He whirled on the piggish-faced man, who also had come up belligerently at his sudden appearance, to stand spread-legged, his own thumbs close to the cartridge belt that circled his ample paunch, a leer on his thick, ugly lips.

"This here game is off," Peep announced decisively. "The kid is drunk—besides, he hasn't any money to lose. That bet he made don't ride."

"The hell it don't." With a sudden movement, the stranger kicked aside his chair, started backing off to swing down into a half crouch, his hand dangerously near the butt of the gun holstered at his hip. "I'd like to know who you are butting in and trying to tell us what to do."

His puzzled gaze darted between Peep and Tommy. It was plain that the striking resemblance between the two had him baffled.

"I'm Peep O'Day, if that means anything to you." Peep's tone was soft, dead, frozen—an ominous warning to men who knew him on the Satanka range. "The guy you couldn't bluff into drinking with you. This kid is my brother. And I'm repeating—that bet don't ride."

"Do you know who you are talking to?" the stranger bellowed.

"No, nor I don't care a damn!"

"I'm Hi Binder!" The heavy-set man's face was contorted with furious rage. "Hi Binder! Do you get that? The hombre every tough jasper from the Bitter Roots to the Sangres has hunted cover from. I'll—"

"You'll bust a hamstring yelling if you aren't careful," Peep snorted disgustedly. "There isn't anybody hunting cover from you around Satanka—least of all me. So get this, cowboy! That bet is off! Do you savvy?"

"I'd like to see you call it off!" Tommy found his voice to put in hotly. "I'll—"

"And I'll back you up in anything you start, kid!" the fellow, Binder, egged him on.

"You don't look tough to anybody but yourself," Peep purred.

Unconsciously his long slim fingers worked along the belt near the holstered forty-one his father had given him. A thrill surged through him, the thrill he had felt in other days when a wild strain had cropped out to start him along the path of whining lead. But—those days were past. He had caught hold of himself. Tommy had taken his place as the crack shot of the Satanka range. Those who knew the two of them had forgotten his skill in their admiration of Tommy's. In fact, in the time that he had toted the old forty-one, he, too, had forgotten. But there had been a time when—

Until the day of his father's death the gun itself had been a thing of mystery. Save for its rounded butt—like that of a dueling-pistol—and a bull's-eye burned on the walnut stock—it was not so much unlike any other six-shooter. Yet, strangely, old Hank had prized it above anything he had possessed. Peep could not recall ever having seen it out of his reach until, with trembling hands, he had passed it over to him on his deathbed.

"It's yours now," he seemed to hear again his father's faltering voice. "I always meant that Tommy should have it, but with that hot head of his it might get him into trouble." Peep had wondered then, wondered now at the strange bequest. His father, too, knew he had not carried a firearm since he had promised Hope that he was through with gun-toting forever. Hope—

The scene on Ragged Hound the morning he had left for round-up recurred. "To be able to shoot like that is a curse, Peep," he heard her saying again.

Then: "That gun never harmed but one human." Old

Hank's words broke in to sear into his memory. "That was before your time. We were pals. Got us Colts just alike. He went bad. Stole some of my critters. They buried him back yonder in the East. Somehow in the fracas we got hold of each other's guns. This is his. You'll find his initials here in this bull's-eye on the butt. You might tangle up with his son some day. Who can tell? You'll know him because his name and initials are just the same as his paw's. I'm hoping you won't, Peep. But you never can tell. It's an odd caliber now—a forty-one. And the cylinder turns backward; but you can still get ca'tridges for it. Swear you'll never use it against any fellow unless he is a rustler—or the son of the hombre I plugged—or—"

The thin voice had faded then into a choking, inaudible whisper. But the grim irony of the thing struck Peep now as it had then. He was face to face with a situation where he must either play the coward or ignore his father's dying wish and shoot a stranger! A coward! He jerked straight—

A threatening twitch of Binder's right hand warned him of his immediate danger. From the corner of eyes focused on Binder he caught a glimpse of confederates edging in.

Came a lull, a sinister tenseness that seemed to paralyze men's limbs and clutch at the muscles of their throats. The Jumbo patrons had melted away. Crowds have a way of sensing tragedy in rangeland.

With only the soft scraping of boots, the tiny tinkle of spur rowels, the punchers were edging back, leaving a lane open between them. The deathlike stillness deepened on the big resort, a stillness so intense that it was palpable. Clock-ticks passed, clock-ticks without breath or noticeable motion. Then—

Binder moved, a lightning fast move that baffled sight. A shot roared through the room. The echo beat down with deafening reverberations on drumming ears. Peep heard the lead whine past his head, heard the bullet *putt* into the wall behind him. He sensed rather than saw Binder, with six companions now about him. And on either side the swimming, set faces of the immobile crowd.

Instinctively he knew that Binder's finger was contracting for a second shot. The mad jumble of thought that started to cascade through his mind ceased as suddenly as it started. His brain became cool and calculating, a thing apart from his body—stony, impervious to excitement, yet throbbing with the hot blood of combat.

His own hand moved—swift as a flutter of light. A gasp whistled through the crowd.

That draw—Binder's had been fast, but Satanka had yet to see a gunman move with the baffling speed Peep O'Day had just shown. There were some who nodded knowingly. They recalled a Peep of five years before, a Peep who split seconds with the best of them.

Came two shots, cracking one on the other. Binder swayed as if in a wind, jerked violently, lurched over, clutched out blindly for the table. Peep gave him but a sweeping glance; he seldom missed. Through the blue smoke swirling ceiling-ward from his hot-barreled forty-one he dared a glance at Tommy. His brother stood clinging to the back of a chair for support. His face was chalk white. For all his bluff he was making no effort to draw.

Peep's glance snapped back to Binder's six companions facing him.

"I got into this for you," he hurled at Tommy through clenched teeth.

"I can't help it," Tommy choked out. "I—I—owe him a thousand dollars." A flood of color lashed his pasty cheeks. "What did you want to butt in for—just when the cards were beginning to break for me—I'd have won it back."

"A thousand dollars!" Peep's violently straining muscles jerked. "A thousand—give me your gun!" Before the nervous Tommy could comply, Peep snatched the weapon from his holster. His voice steadied, cracked like a blacksnake in the silence that now was tangible. "Find Hope. Tell her it's too bad to start out tonight. Get out of here as quick as you know how—but don't try to go to the T-7 until morning."

"Naw, you don't," bawled the deathly white Binder, letting go his hold on the table to claw madly at a hairy forearm from which blood was spurting. "He owes me a thousand bucks. I'm going to collect."

"Collect from me!" Peep shot back. "He's going. Travel, Tommy. But don't start out with Hope."

"The hell I won't!" Tommy spun about dizzily and ducked into the crowd. "I'll take her now just to show you you're not running me."

The words boomed in Peep's drumming ears. Yet in the stunning excitement they seemed far away, although apparently his mind was never clearer, nor his nerves steadier. His full gaze swept around to Binder and his gangsters who waited like men transfixed, making no move to carry on the fight.

As he stood poised, motionless as stone, every muscle taut, straining, there came to him one of those inane flashes men sometimes experience in moments of danger— a reckless impulse to tear his gaze from his opponents and see the initials his father had told him were burned in the bull's-eye on the stock of the forty-one clutched in his hand. Strange he had not thought of them before—when he had ample time without deliberately inviting—

He tried to dismiss the crazy notion. The longer the deadly pantomime continued the more persistent that notion became. At last he could stifle it no longer. Realizing full well the consequences of tearing his eyes, even for an instant, from those burning gazes, he risked a look—a swift darting glance. Yet it found the initials old Hank had said belonged to the man he had shot—and to his son.

J.T.

In the excitement of the moment he could not recall

anyone he had ever known with the initials J.T. Still, they did ring strangely familiar. Thoughts flashed, cinema-like, through his mind. Tumbling, riotous thoughts, thoughts of a lifetime, crowded into a moment. Then suddenly a desire to have done with Binder and his gang without further trouble possessed him. Somewhere outside in the storm was Tommy—Tommy, recklessly drunk, starting on a dangerous road with Hope! He must stop them at any cost.

He took a step backward. The seven who faced him shifted nervously. Another step! From somewhere came a shot. It was beating down deafeningly from the raftered ceiling.

Came a fusillade. Into Peep's swiftly functioning yet cloudy brain flashed the knowledge that Binder and his companions had opened up. Bullets were whistling about his ears. Glasses were splintering along the back-bar. The mirror was crashing into millions of blinding crystals to slice the air. Bottles were popping. Corks were flying. The big saloon was a bedlam of sound, yet strangely, ominously silent.

Then in a flash his brain was clear again. Scorching blood began cascading through his veins, hammered in his eardrums. Before he was aware of it, the forty-one and the gun he had snatched from Tommy's holster were belching a deadly stream into the crew.

Through eyes that looked and saw red he was conscious of them breaking for cover, was vaguely aware that from behind the stove and poker tables they were pumping back lead at him. The acrid blue smoke, swirling ceiling-ward from hot-barreled guns, blinded him. But his actions too were blind, mechanical, had no connection with his muscle-taut body. His forty-one sent a man into the air. A bloodcurdling scream arose above the bedlam. The fellow spun completely about, pitched headlong to the floor. At the instant a ripping pain smashed the forty-one from fingers that suddenly went dead. Peep stooped for it. The panic-stricken crowd surged forward. It was kicked from his reach. The gun he had taken from Tommy snapped on an exploded cartridge.

"I'm out of ca'tridges," he shouted recklessly. "But we'll meet again."

In three great backward bounds he was at the door, had wrenched it open. A burly man bolted in at the moment, blocked his retreat.

"Get that walloper," Binder bawled out. "He's killed our pard. Don't let him get out."

"Tommy O'Day!" The exclamation burst from the lips of the newcomer, who stood peering at Peep through the smoke-dimmed light. It was Bud Hamby, sheriff of Satanka. The gunfire ceased. Peep's mind worked like lightning. To set the officer right as to his identity, and submit to arrest, would mean that he could not be near Hope in case she needed him. If he had the night to follow her, to see that she arrived safely at the T-7, he could return on the morrow and—

A resolution formed in his whirling brain, a resolution not to correct Hamby's mistake, one often made on the Satanka range. Many times he was mistaken for Tommy; now that resemblance served him well. To continue the deception meant that if he could temporarily give the officer the slip, Hamby would arrest Tommy and hold him—at least until his brother sobered up. Meanwhile he could see Hope and warn her of the danger of attempting to make the T-7 before morning. After that he could surrender.

"I'll take the blame for this killing, Bud," he said coolly, facing about. "I'll be at the jail tomorrow—but I'm going now."

"Like hell you are!" Hamby whipped out his Colt. "If that hombre is dead, it's murder. You can't even get bond. Hand over your gun—I'll have to lock you up—now,

Tommy."

"That ain't Tommy," the pain-torn Binder found voice to bellow. But his words were drowned in the uproar that suddenly burst forth in the Jumbo to rise in a crescendoing roar.

Hamby's gun swung up. Peep's fist shot out, knocked the Colt from the officer's hand. He bundled taut muscles and charged through the door.

Once outside, he swept the street in a single glance. It was deserted. Through the drizzle he glimpsed a buckboard just pulling away from the livery barn. He shook himself, bounded across the sodden walk, raced for the string of horses tied at the hitch rail. He jerked loose the reins of the nearest, vaulted into the saddle. His slashing rowels lifted the brute. It plowed a lane through its mates, gained the center of the slippery street in a single lunge.

From the Jumbo arose a clamor. Shouts, curses, the wild cracking of six-shooters—orange powder-flame laced the twilight gloom. The air was full of lead. A bullet pierced Peep's hat. He crouched low in the wet saddle and gave his mount rein. It ran like a thoroughbred in the treacherous footing. The yelling crowd tumbled from the saloon. Other guns came into play. To no avail. Peep dashed past the livery barn at breakneck speed. Ahead, through the rain, he could see the buckboard, an indistinct hulk in the gathering darkness. His spurs were lashing viciously. The horse plunged on. As he came abreast of the buckboard a mighty shout roared down the street.

"Stop that fellow! Stop Tommy O'Day! He's killed a jasper in the Jumbo; done murder!" It was Hamby's voice. Even at the distance, even above the pounding hoofs in the sticky mud it beat on Peep's madly drumming ears.

He raced by the buckboard, caught a glimpse of Hope's white face. Dark as it was, for an instant their eyes seemed to meet. Her head seemed to go up defiantly. Then he had flashed past, was lost in the rain-drenched prairies; a sudden prey to the soul-sickening torment that comes of spilling human blood; a victim of a conscience that cried out against the injustice he had done Tommy, his brother; an outlaw on the fugitive trail.

Through the sluicing roar of his own hot blood in his ears a question hammered to the rhythm of the thundering hoofs: *Am I my brother's keeper? Am I my brother's keeper?* Always the answer came back in the faltering voice of his father: "You—are—his—keeper—Peep—like—the—Good—Book—says—"

Chapter Nine

STORM ON THE PRAIRIE

THE MURKY TWILIGHT THICKENED into even murkier night. The wind came up in howling gusts, driving the rain in sheets before it to turn the prairies into a brimming sea of mud and water. New storms rolling out of the west burst with deafening crashes of thunder. The din was awful, terrifying. Peal followed peal until they mingled in one continuous roar that seemed to rock the flats. Vivid flashes of lightning tore the sky, burned blindingly for an instant, then vanished to leave an impenetrable blackness. The air was heavy with the stench of sulphur, of sun-seared greasewood sodden now and dripping.

Unmindful of the flying mud and water that covered him from head to foot, Peep roweled on recklessly. The wild running of the horse seemed to ease the violence of emotions that held him prey. He gave no thought to being overtaken by a posse. Few men would risk putting a mount over the slippery flats at such a pace as he was setting. Few horses could be made to face the driving rain as his mount was doing, its nose and tail on a level, ears plastered back, great muscles pushing the miles behind with an ease that seemed to leave it floating, touching the slippery ground with a lightness that kept it foot sure. Added to this, the downpour, which human eye could scarcely penetrate, was in his favor.

Enveloping darkness closed in about him. The prairies became a Stygian, storm-swept void. He eased in his running mount to slacken its speed without throwing it off balance on the treacherous ground. When it had slowed down to a trot, he pulled off to one side of the road, a wan streak of color in the gloom. There he shifted sidewise in his saddle, weight in one stirrup, working his arms to keep warm.

Life sure is a funny proposition, he mused philosophically. *For five years I've gone straight as a string. Comes a day when I want to show up at my best—what do I do? Start raisin' hell. What does Hope—* He groaned aloud and startled his horse, which flicked its ears angrily but was blowing too hard to do more than snort with fright. *And to think, I did that shooting with Paw's forty-one! After I'd promised him I'd never— After I'd promised Hope—* He worked beneath his slicker and dragged the gun from its holster. He stared at it strangely in the darkness. The heft of it, the stock—it was Tommy's forty-five. In the excitement he had forgotten that he'd dropped the old curved-butt forty-one, with the bull's-eye, in the Jumbo. "It's just as well," he muttered. "I hate to lose it, because it was Paw's. But if it is going to get me into trouble every time I tote it, I reckon I'm better off without it."

He twisted in the saddle, hunched about until the driving rain was pelting against his back. The movement set a sharp pain to stabbing his hand. Not until then did he realize that he was wounded. The bullet that had knocked the forty-one from his grasp had creased his fingers. Now that he was aware of it, the injury began to throb with sickening regularity.

Minutes dragged by with nerve-wracking slowness; the crash of thunder, the hiss of the rain, the howling of the wind—eerie and awful in the dripping greasewood—joined in a tumult that barely died before it began again with the boom of new thunderclaps.

Then, after an infinity of time, his straining ears caught the sound of galloping hoofs.

That will be Hamby, he decided grimly. *Wonder how he came to pass Tommy up?*

He waited with bated breath, but without sighting him the posse sloshed on down the road, huge misshapen objects, to be swallowed up quickly in the roaring storm. After they had passed he roweled his protesting mount nearer to the trail. It moved with its rump low, its hind legs bent, elastic against the stinging drops. The hulking buckboard burst out of the gloom, directly before him. Jerking up, he strained to hear above the sudden beating of his heart that seemed to grow more audible as he subdued his breath to listen.

Presently he caught Tommy's voice, raised, furious with anger. "And to think he'd lie and get me in bad just to save his own neck."

The words crashed down with the force of a blow upon Peep.

"It will come out all right, Tommy—" It was Hope's voice. At sound of it, Peep's heart bounded from the depths of despair into which his brother's censure had forced it. "You lied just as he did. What did you want to tell the sheriff you were Peep for?"

"Because there wasn't anything else to do," Tommy's snarling answer came to the straining Peep, who was rigid in his stirrups now, listening. "If I had told him I was Tommy he would have arrested me and made me go back to Satanka for a shooting I didn't even—"

"I can't understand it." Hope's voice grew fainter as they wallowed on down the road. "It is so unlike Peep. And—" Peep leaned forward in his saddle, hanging breathlessly onto her every word. "And he—you remember, he once quit carrying a gun—before I left. I can't imagine Peep O'Day killing a man—now. Why did he do it?"

"Because the old saying, 'Still water runs deep,' isn't very far off, I reckon," was Tommy's malicious rejoinder.

The insinuation was plainer to Peep than if his brother had answered Hope's question. The underhand thrust, the evil intent of the statement, lashed him into a momentary fury. But he stifled it quickly, conquered a wild impulse to overtake them, choke a retraction from Tommy's lips.

But what did it matter, after all. Hope no doubt despised him now. After he had seen them safely to the T-7 he probably never would meet her, never so much as lay eyes on her again. He was an outlaw, doomed to the outlaw trail, an outcast. The thought brought his teeth together with a click, his lips but narrow lines, grimly set.

Touching his pony with the rowels, he moved forward, crowding as closely to the buckboard as he dared without being observed. How long he rode thus, his ears closed to the fragmentary conversation that drifted back, his mind awhirl with thoughts that churned endlessly and without meaning through it, he did not know, or care. He jerked straight in his saddle as a bolt of lightning ripped open the sky, sizzled like a fuse, and streaked vividly to the ground to burst like a mighty grenade before him. A crash of thunder blasted the heavens, rolled on and on until it died to an ominous growl in the distance.

Half blinded by the bolt, that plainly had struck somewhere on the prairie just ahead, Peep jerked straight in his saddle, strove to pierce the gloom. A sound like a scream had echoed the thunderclap. The buckboard, which he had managed to keep within his line of vision, suddenly had become a mass without form. And in a flash it was lost in the darkness.

Peep lifted his mount into a mud-slinging lunge with his rowels. It was gone in a furious burst of speed. A short distance and it slid to its haunches, spraddled forelegs plowing furrows in the sodden earth, snorts whistling through flaring nostrils. Directly ahead Peep made out a dark object. He leaped down. Holding tightly to the bridle reins of the brute, which tried frantically to tear from his grasp, he stooped. He lifted the unconscious, mud-splattered form of Hope Thompson into his arms.

"My hunch was right," he muttered. "The team ran away, just as I figured it would in a storm like this, and threw her out. If Tommy gets the brutes stopped between here and the T-7 he is plumb lucky."

Holding the girl tightly in his arms, he tried to mount. The terrified horse lunged and shied, refused stubbornly to let him come near with the inert figure. Finally, after several attempts, he succeeded in checking the snorting brute and twisting its head about until its nose was at the stirrup and it had smelled of the motionless form. The pony quieted for a moment. With a strength born of desperation, Peep snapped into the saddle. Shielding the unconscious girl with his body, Peep started forward, the horse sidling along uneasily under its double load.

Chapter Ten

HIS BROTHER'S KEEPER

A MILE OR MORE FARTHER ALONG THE ROAD, without sight of Tommy or the buckboard—which he expected to run onto at any moment, a tangled mass of wreckage—another dazzling bolt of lightning shivered across the sky, leaving a chasm of blinding light behind it. The angry growl of thunder increased in violence, ending in a terrific clap that seemed to split his eardrums and leave them ringing. A temporary lull, an awesome stillness followed the report. Then the storm burst with renewed fury, whipping slicing torrents into his face and bringing the horse about, rump to the howling wind. For all he could do, Peep could no longer make the brute head into the downpour. It was sawing on the bridle reins, fighting its head savagely. The instinct of a rangeman told him that for all the darkness, for all the raging storm, the brute knew what it was about, knew that the way they were taking was not right.

With the torrent the girl stirred in Peep's numbed arms. Greatly relieved that the dead weight had shifted, he gave the horse loose rein. It left the road immediately and plunged out onto the flats. His sense of direction told Peep that the animal was heading south. For the first time there came to him a flash of wonder at whose horse he had taken from the hitch rail at the Jumbo. But having no way of knowing, he had no alternative but to let it take its course, for hampered by the girl in his arms, he could not force it along the road to the T-7. Sooner or later, he knew it would bring him to where it belonged.

Again the inert form shifted. This time with a movement that told him she had returned to consciousness.

"Are you all right, Hope?" he whispered in her ear.

"Yes, Tommy, thank you," wearily. "What—happened?"

Tommy! A protest sprang to Peep's lips. It was on his tongue to tell her that it was he—Peep—not Tommy, that he had followed her through the storm, lied about his identity to be near her for just such an emergency as had arisen, but—

"You had a mighty narrow squeeze," he found himself saying huskily after a time. "That lightning bolt which struck out yonder in the greasewood somewhere scared the team. The broncs ran away. I—I—" His inane floundering made his ears burn. "I—stopped them after a while. Cut one of them loose and let the other one go." He gulped the finish of the falsehood.

He could feel her steady gaze through the darkness.

"But—the—saddle?" she asked through teeth chattering with cold.

"Oh—I—I had it in the buckboard under a trap," he lied, thankful for the gloom that concealed his burning face.

"Oh!" Her stifled exclamation for a moment made him fearful that she had not been deceived. "It—it's funny Jim would have a runaway team broke to the saddle, isn't it?"

The accusation, veiled in the form of a question, nonplused him. It was an unwritten law on the T-7 that no horse ever put under harness was to be ridden. Peep cursed himself inwardly for an idiot. But he held his tongue, fearful of another break, occupied in peering ahead at the vivid slashes of lightning which stabbed the ebony sky. Silence fell between them as the pony splashed across the prairies, a silence that presently became acutely embarrassing, that required explanation, but for which there seemed none.

After a seeming infinity of time, the horse stopped of its own accord.

"Now where are we?" Peep asked, thankful for any respite from that awful silence. "This horse has brought us somewhere, but where I haven't the slightest notion."

When the animal refused to budge under the rowels, he tightened his hold on the girl, swung down, and placed her on her feet. She stood swaying weakly against him. With one hand he found the latigo, loosened it, dragged the sodden saddle from the dripping animal's back. Tossing it into a thicket of brush, with the cantle up to protect the skirts, he dragged off the saddle blanket. Stripping off his slicker, he threw it about Hope, placed the saddle blanket on the ground and forced her gently onto it. Then, securing the throw rope from the saddle bow, he staked out the horse to a clump of greasewood and removed the bit from its mouth. This done, he stumbled around in the gloom, trying desperately to get his bearings.

Directly ahead he came on a deep wash, which the wary horse had refused to cross. Half-blind exploration revealed that it was partly protected by an overhanging bank. Going back to the girl, he helped her to her feet, secured the saddle blanket, and half carried, half dragged her to the shelter. There he made her comfortable, the blanket beneath her shivering form, which was completely enveloped in his great slicker.

"Reckon, if you don't mind, I'll nose around and see if I can find out where we are," he suggested. "I haven't any dry matches or I'd build you a fire. But—I ought to get the lay of the land in a few minutes, then—"

"Tommy, what do you suppose became of Peep?" she surprised him by asking. "I'm afraid he'll get—be killed riding so recklessly in this storm. He went by us at such a wild pace."

"Don't worry about Peep." He strove to keep his voice steady. "He'll take care of himself. And I reckon when everything comes out he won't be as worthless and undeserving as he seems right now." The last slipped out unintentionally, a defense of himself that he could not stifle.

Of all persons, to have Hope Thompson thinking that he—

"What's the use of trying to deceive me any longer, Peep?" she asked quietly.

"You—know—me?" he blurted out incredulously.

"Certainly. Why not?"

"But—but—how?"

"Because— Oh, just something—I just know you are Peep, that's all," desperately. "When you said you had cut loose one of Jim's driving-horses and were riding it, I was convinced you were lying. You know as well as I do Jim never had an animal broke to the harness and the saddle too. Why did you try to make me think you were Tommy?"

"Because—because—" Peep floundered hopelessly. "I— Well, I reckon I was afraid you'd be scared with a—a killer," he managed to get out.

"But, Peep!" She sprang to her feet and seized hold of his arm. "You're not a killer. Tell me you are not. Please do."

"I can't," he returned bitterly. "I can't—Hope."

"Why did you do it?" There was a queer catch in her voice that cut him deeply.

His heart commanded that he reveal the whole story. But Tommy—Old Hank— His swiftly working mind framed the answer he voiced even before he was aware of what he was saying.

"I reckon it was because I'm just plumb bad," he muttered savagely.

She let go of his arm, drew away from him. He was conscious of the shudder that racked her.

"But you promised you'd never use that gun again as you did. Is your word so easily broken?"

He was at a loss to answer this. He wanted to tell her the whole story. His soul cried out that he tell her. She knew Thompson had ordered him to carry the gun. But

Thompson had not ordered him to draw it in a saloon brawl he might easily have avoided. Yet for Tommy's sake— He rebelled at the idea of further implicating himself—or Tommy.

"Some day, mebbeso I can explain, Hope," he told her contritely. "But right now, I can't. If you want to, you can trust me—I'd like to have you. But if not—"

"I might have stood it all—still maintained my trust in you if you hadn't blamed Tommy for that shooting, Peep," she cried. "Why did you do such a cowardly thing? It is so unlike—"

"So I could follow you to the T-7 in case anything happened," he muttered. "Hamby mistook me for Tommy— I let him keep on thinking I was him so he would pick Tommy up and hold him. That way Tommy couldn't have started out in this storm with you. I warned him—I was only trying to protect— But Tommy was too smart for me. I heard him say he told Hamby he was me."

"Then you really were—you really were trying to help me." There was a queer note he could not fathom in her voice, a strange, unexplainable note that thrilled him, yet left him dead with the thought she knew him to be a liar. "They were shooting at you there on the street at Satanka. Suppose they had killed you?"

"Suppose they had?" was his grim response. "I don't reckon anybody would have cared a heap."

"Don't you dare say that, Peep O'Day," she flashed. "I—I—"

"Well, they wouldn't have, would they?" he persisted, secretly delighted in the defense he had aroused within her.

But his spirits dashed suddenly. To his dismay he was conscious of her shrinking in the darkness. He heard her moving away. He followed to find her huddled back beneath the cutbank.

He jerked straight. "I'll scout around," he said. "I'll be

THE LONG ROPE 79

back as soon as I find out where we are."

"You don't need to hurry," she threw after him, a tear in her voice, he thought. "I can take care of myself. And I can find my way back home as soon as it gets daylight. It isn't the first prairie thunderstorm I've weathered. Nor it won't be the last."

"Now what the hell have I said to rile her like that," he mumbled to himself as he sloshed away into the darkness.

Chapter Eleven

THE HIDDEN CABIN

IT WAS ALMOST AN HOUR LATER when, after endless floundering through ravines which ran ankle-deep with water and fighting his way up and down the slippery sides of innumerable coulees, Peep swung about and started to retrace his course to the cutbank where he had left the girl. Hope of finding out where he was before daylight appeared useless. His aimless wandering had revealed nothing, only reduced him to a state of numbing weariness. His muscles ached with cold and fatigue and were on the point of rebelling at further punishment. Added to this was the haunting sensation of being walled in by a darkness that not only seemed to suffocate him with its intensity but made all direction the same. For the first time in his life he was forced to admit that he was lost. And lost in a country every mile of which he had known since childhood.

By now the storm had swept on past, leaving in its wake a steady drizzle that drenched his already sodden clothes, chilled him like frost to the marrow, made his brush-scarred leather chaps hang like shackles about his hips. Thunder rumbled and muttered on the horizon like the roar of a distant surf. The flashes of lightning only served to intensify the darkness after they had vanished. Yet having, with the instinct of a range-bred man, held as nearly as possible to a straight line from where he had left Hope, he plodded along the back trail.

"Wouldn't that frost you?" he muttered. "I'll bet that jug-headed horse I rode belongs to somebody who hangs out around hereabouts. But who?" When no answer was forthcoming to the baffling question, he plowed on doggedly. The sticky gumbo clotted his rowels, rolled up under his boots until he could scarcely drag his feet. The rain clung like ice to his shivering form. "If that brute didn't bring me to its home, or somewhere close, it's the first range horse I ever turned loose in a storm that wouldn't."

He pondered the thing as he lumbered along, stubbornly refusing to give in to his aching fatigue, pausing only at intervals to catch his rasping breath or kick the gumbo from his boots, when they became too heavy to lift.

"It beats the devil as long as I have lived in this country that I can still get lost," he panted. "I thought—" He drew up sharply to get control of his heaving breath. Below, he sensed rather than saw the vast hollowness of a deep canyon. About him were towering rocks, indistinct, misshapen in the darkness—rimrock above the Stygian abyss. "I know we haven't come more than ten miles off the Surprise Creek-Satanka road," he reasoned. "And near as I can figure out we've been traveling south—"

Using his dripping hat to shield his straining eyes from the pelting drops, he peered about in the blackness.

"Hell!" he blurted out suddenly. "I'm in the foothill brakes just east of the Flying Spear. I can't be any place else. I must have got hold of a horse that didn't know where he was going and didn't care a damn—just drifted ahead of the storm. But I never heard of—"

For all his conclusion, he could not reconcile the fact that a horse, like a pigeon, will take the straightest course home once it has free rein. The strange animal he had ridden so precipitately out of Satanka had seemed intelligent—an unusually fine horse the way it had run and stood up under the grueling pace he had set, and utterly dependable. Horses as a rule in rangeland were to be trusted, yet—

Rid at last of the haunting sensation of not knowing where he was, once he had gotten his bearings, he set out again at a surer pace along the rim of the canyon. But he had gone only a short distance when a glow far below, and almost concealed under an overhanging ledge, caught his eye and brought him to an abrupt halt.

"Wonder who would have a campfire clear back in these brakes?" he said aloud, after the manner of men of the silent trails who frame many of their thoughts in words. "And on a night like this. . . . But at least it would be some place to dry out."

He started on only to stop again, prey to a harassing uncertainty. He wanted to return to Hope and get her to shelter as quickly as possible. He knew that his own ranch, the Flying Spear, was not more than five miles to the westward from the point where he suddenly had gotten his bearings. However, sight of the light in the wild brakes, where there were no ranches, and which were seldom entered except by cowboys in search of strays, had aroused his curiosity. If he left the place, there was little likelihood that he could find it again in the jumble of badlands. Yet to go into the canyon would require considerable time. He lingered on hesitatingly, humped shivering against the drizzle, teeth chattering.

Determined presently to investigate the strange light even though it meant delay in returning to Hope, he scouted around in the darkness until he found a cow trail —a murky ribbon a little lighter than the other soggy earth—winding down through the rimrocks. Cautiously he started the slippery descent. For all his care, the going was difficult. Again and again he lost his footing to stumble and fall to his knees, only to get up and plunge on. The drizzle struck him full in the face, blinded him. He was mud from head to foot. In spite of the violent exertion he shivered with cold and fatigue.

After what seemed hours of toil, he reached the bottom of the canyon and went forward. Rounding a bend, he almost ran headlong into a cabin that stood directly in his path. Even in the darkness he knew by the wan color of the logs that they had been freshly peeled and the building erected recently. He moved about stealthily, searching for the light he had seen from above. But it had vanished as completely as though by a trick of legerdemain. And the cabin itself seemed to be unoccupied. He was almost on the point of trying the door when his quick ear, tuned to every vibration of rangeland, caught the sound of hoofbeats above the swishing of the storm. Presently the hoofbeats became those of a single horse, sloshing wearily through the mud.

His nerves suddenly tight with expectancy, alert against some unknown danger, Peep hugged the side of the building and waited breathlessly. The creak of saddle leather became more distinct. A pony passed so close to him that he could hear it blowing, hear the tinkle of spur rowels, the champing of bit steel. Yet the rider was only a blurred and shapeless mass in the gloom beneath the canyon's rim.

The horseman rode directly to the door of the cabin. Stirrups squeaked as his weight left the saddle. A few heavy, uncertain steps. Then the strange night rider seemed to be fumbling with a padlock.

"Somebody must have busted the hasp," Peep heard him mutter sourly.

From within came the bang of an overturned chair, the sudden uneasy shuffle of feet. Peep caught the movement of the newcomer as he leaped back. The door was opened the width of a crack. A pencil of light stabbed the gloom.

"Who's there?" a harsh unfriendly voice demanded.

Peep strained for a glimpse of the speaker, peering through the partly opened door. Recognition, even in the wan light, struck him with the force of a mighty blow. It was Hi Binder, his opponent across the poker table in the Jumbo saloon at Satanka. One of the fellow's arms was done in a sling. A dully glinting blue-barreled gun was clutched in his good hand.

A clock-tick of silence, strained silence filled with ominous portent. Then from the darkness:

"Who the hell are you and what are you doing in my cabin?"

"Your cabin nothing," Binder's voice came back snarlingly. "I guess there isn't any law against a jasper drying out on a night like this, is there? Climb down off your high horse, stranger. Light and come on in and thaw out."

At the newcomer's first words, Peep jerked with muscular violence. He did not need to see this lone rider of the storm-swept trails to know who it was. For framed now in the path of light from the doorway stood big Jim Thompson!

The clump of heavy boots, the jangle of rowels. The door banged shut on his huge gaunt frame. The light obscured, the darkness became more Stygian, defied the sight of eyes accustomed for a moment to light. When Peep again could make out the indistinct form of things about him, he moved cautiously around to the door, laid an ear against it. But the sound of voices from within came to him only in muffled undertones.

Chapter Twelve

ONE MOMENT TOO LATE

FOR A SEEMING INFINITY OF TIME Peep prowled stealthily around the strange building, wondering what had become of the light he had seen from the rim of the canyon above. But there was no trace of it. The canyon was enveloped in an awesome darkness. If the cabin so much as had windows they were tightly boarded up and the logs closely chinked.

After several futile attempts to overhear what the group within was saying—and the overturned chair and shuffling of feet at Thompson's approach led him to believe there were several inside—he gave up and started away. Discovery of the cabin, which until now—in spite of the many times he had ridden the canyon—he did not even know existed, filled him with a disquieting wonder. It was a foreman's duty to know every place on his range that would house man or beast. Only those who sought absolute privacy from prying eyes would build deep in such a wild canyon fastness. Yet he never before had run across it. His men, who rode constantly, had made no mention of it, which made him positive that his punchers were as much in the dark concerning it as he was himself.

Thompson's angry question of Binder's occupancy of the shack increased his perplexity. Jim had told him back in Satanka that he was going up the Belle Fourche river on a hunt for rustlers. Yet here he was alone, in the dead of a storm-ridden night, within ten miles of the T-7 and in the opposite direction from that which he said he would take. Peep recalled that the cowman had made it clear he intended to stop at various ranches in hope of obtaining some information that would lead to identifying the cattle thieves. But why had he ridden to this mystery cabin and informed Binder that it belonged to him? The window-less shack deep in the canyon itself certainly was not an abode of honest-dealing citizens. Nor could he understand why, if Thompson had built it for a line camp, as his de-mand would indicate, he had never mentioned it to the foreman of the T-7, or to any of his punchers.

The glimpse he had gotten of Binder's ugly countenance through the doorway added nothing to his calm. The sud-den reappearance of the fellow, he tried to convince him-self, was due only to chance. He did not know where the piggish-faced man and his pals belonged, but no doubt after the fight in the saloon they too had started for their homes—wherever they were—had gotten off the trail as he himself had done in the storm, and stumbled onto this cabin.

It occurred to Peep that the place might even be Bind-er's hang-out. This conjecture was strengthened by a sud-den notion that sprang into his mind. The horse he had taken from in front of the Jumbo belonged to one of Binder's men. Its movements unhampered by rein, the brute had done its utmost to bring Hope and himself through the storm to the lonely cabin. But why had Bind-er, a stranger on the Satanka range, dared question the ownership of Jim Thompson, who, even though he plain-ly had failed to mention this particular cabin, had line shacks strung the length and breadth of the country?

Setting a pace equal to his tumultuous thoughts, Peep found the trail where he had made the descent and toiled back up the slippery side of the canyon, clinging to rocks and trees to maintain a precarious footing. After a time he reached the rimrock. Stopping only long enough to catch his breath and gather some loose stones, which he heaped together for a marker, he stumbled along toward where he had left Hope.

"I've got a hunch that place will bear watching," he

muttered, pausing after a time in a break in the rimrock to look below. "And I'll just keep an eye peeled for the shebang." As he stood, the mystery of the light he had seen suddenly was explained. What he had mistaken for a campfire was the chimney of a fireplace, which gave forth a shower of sparks each time the blaze was replenished.

About to go on again, a muffled shot burst on his straining eardrums. A fusillade rattled an echo which slapped back and forth between the canyon walls. Jets of orange powder-flame laced the darkness of the abyss.

The firing ceased as suddenly as it had begun. A vast stillness, like that found in chambers of the dead, settled down.

"It will be old Jim in a ruckus," Peep growled. "I reckon he needs help." He dragged the forty-five from its water-logged holster, only to recall that it was empty. Yet in spite of it, he was running back through the darkness toward the head of the trail. Regardless of the fact that he was unarmed, he started down just as the thud of hoofbeats below pounded into the night. A few scattered shots, a volley of oaths ascended. He caught a shout—in Thompson's angry, bellowing voice—with amazing clearness.

"I'm warning you to make tracks or I'll bring in my punchers and smoke you out!"

"Well, old Jim is still kicking," Peep muttered, halting in his precipitate descent, and turning back up the canyon. "That don't sound much like he needs any help now. And I reckon we'll do just what Jim says—show Mister Binder where to head in as quick as we can get the boys rounded up."

"Bring on your hombres!" a taunting yell from Binder drifted up to him. "You can't come up here and shoot one of my men and get away with it, you—"

Peep stopped as though transfixed.

"Shoot one of my men!"

What did Binder mean? Had Jim Thompson— But the question only again set the crazy chain of problems, which cried for solution, churning through his mind. He strained to listen. Deep foreboding silence had fallen again on the canyon. The hoofbeats of a single horse had died to a throb on the distant night air. He started once again the toiling ascent of the canyon side.

As he plodded along, the events since the moment he had drawn against Binder and his gang in the Jumbo stalked in review through his mind. Suddenly a mental picture of the Colt his father had given him appeared before him. The initials on the stock—as he had seen them in that daring, foolhardy glance in the Jumbo—flashed before his eyes. They had stood out so vividly they now seemed to sear themselves into his brain. Those initials had been—

"J.T.," he blurted out breathlessly. "Hell, there is only one jasper in this country with those initials. It's Jim Thompson!"

Dumbfounded by the startling conclusion, he plunged on, scarcely aware that he was running. Old Hank, his father, had admitted killing the father of a man with the initials of J.T. Was that man Jim Thompson? If so, why hadn't old Hank—

The more his thoughts ran riot the faster he moved, giving no thought to time or distance. Time and again he was forced to pull up to catch the breath that rasped in his throat. Now he was trotting through rimrock. Now he had an open stretch where he could make time until he was forced to stop and scrape off the rolling gumbo which gathered like a leaden weight on his boots. Alternately running and walking, after a seemingly endless period of time he came to the cutbank where he had left Hope. Yet his brain still swirled with the baffling problems. And he was no nearer a solution to those questions than he had been beside the cabin deep in the canyon.

"Are you all right, Hope?" he called softly as he approached.

"If being nearly frozen is all right, I am," her answer came back through chattering teeth. "Did you find out where we are?"

"Five miles east of the Flying Spear." He rounded the end of the cutbank, sloshed through a gully and was beside her, peering down at her in the darkness. "I reckon I can pick up a cow-trail that will take us that far. I don't think there is a chance to make the T-7 until daylight. What do you say we drag it for the Spear? We can build a fire and get warm. As soon as it is light enough we'll go on to—"

He seemed to feel her eyes searching his face in the gloom.

"I guess that is the only thing to do," she agreed, grudgingly he thought. "I certainly don't care about staying here any longer. And especially alone. But if we can make the Flying Spear, I don't see why we can't go on to the—"

"We can," he cut her short abruptly. "I just thought the Spear would be easier, that you might like to get warm and dry." A bitter note crept into his voice. "I'd forgotten —that—you might be afraid to be out with a—killer."

"I'm not afraid of you any more than I ever was, Peep O'Day," she retorted angrily. "And let me tell you something else. I'm not satisfied by a long ways that there isn't something that you haven't told me behind all this—this trouble of yours. I'll go to the Flying Spear—or any place else with you—gladly."

Her outburst dumbfounded him. He thrilled at her willingness to go with him, yet he was conscious of a dismal sense of shame at his deceit. He made no reply, because no reply he could frame seemed adequate. He reached out in the darkness, found her arm, and silently helped her to her feet. Then he took the saddle blanket and re-saddled the weary pony, which, instead of attempting to graze, stood where it had stopped, its weight resting on three legs, rump to the storm.

"You're going to do the riding," he announced shortly, jerking up the latigo, trying the tightness of the cinch with the horn, and leading the snorting horse as near as he could to the cutbank. "There is some mighty treacherous country between here and home."

"And I'm going to do nothing of the kind," she replied, springing across the muddy coulee and joining him. "You're tired out now. You must be after your walk; you've been gone for hours. If that horse can't keep its footing carrying double it will just have to roll down the hills." He was vividly conscious of her hand on his soaked sleeve. "It wouldn't be the first time we'd been spilled riding a horse double either, would it, Peep?"

A choking catch came into his throat. It was that camaraderie he had found so charming in Hope in the old days. It was the willingness to share anything.

Came to him again an impelling urge to tell her the truth of the whole affair, to exonerate himself, and leave it to her to decide the full measure of his guilt. Yet, as before, something held him silent—the silence of the grim-lipped Peep O'Day, who asked no confidence and gave none—even to the girl that he—

Without a word he caught her by the waist and swung her lightly into the saddle. It was a privilege of other days, yet now— His hands tingled at the contact. Once she was aboard, he vaulted up behind, and still in silence, pricked the pony in the flanks with his rowels. It made a few half-hearted lunges, then with ears plastered back angrily it sidled forward into the darkness.

As they rode, the animal moving at a snail's pace and picking its own way under loose rein, the silence deepened between them. Down the slippery trail he himself had left, instinct guided the horse. Into the rimrock above the canyon they came, he stubbornly refusing to talk, she knowing not what to say. Her muteness filled him with fear. Yet he refused to let it disturb him. His own constant striving to sift coherence from the endless jumble of questions racing through his mind kept him occupied.

At a point where he thought again he could sight the light below in the canyon he pulled up. But only darkness filled the abyss. He goaded the pony—still angry and moving gingerly with its double weight—along again. Nor did he mention to Hope the incident of Thompson and Binder, choosing in his own taciturn way to ferret the thing out for himself.

Time dragged on endlessly, while the cautiously moving and sure-footed pony sloshed through the rimrock. Then they were going down, the brute almost on its rump, Peep himself holding onto the reins above the freezing hand of the girl. The contact apparently held no thrill for her, while he was all too vividly conscious of it.

Then the horse had straightened out and was moving with surer gait, although it was fighting its head savagely to turn back. But Peep held it to a steady course, instinct telling him the route that they now were following led to the Flying Spear. Through the darkness they rode, neither knowing what the other was thinking.

Then presently out of the gloom loomed the barns of the Flying Spear like hideous creatures of a nightmare. Black as it was, Peep recognized them. When the pony stopped of a sudden, he got down stiffly and dropped the barbed-wire gate. He did not bother to replace it, but he led the brute on to the barn. Without a word he helped the girl to dismount and pushed her under shelter.

"Feels good to get out of the rain, doesn't it?" she essayed through chattering teeth, as she huddled in the barn.

"It sure does," he agreed. "I'll have a fire going in a jiffy for you." Unsaddling, he heaped the pony's manger with hay, wiped its quivering body with a gunnysack before they started together for the ranchhouse.

They had taken scarcely a dozen steps when he stopped abruptly, seized hold of the girl and jerked her back roughly. The night was suddenly filled with the drum of running hoofs. A horse lunged past them into the darkness, so close that its pounding hoofs splattered them with mud and water. Voices were upraised and the thunder of other hoofs rose from the direction of the house. Peep pulled Hope deeper into the shadow of the barn.

"Let him go!" someone shouted. "We'll get him later."

"Who—is—it—Peep?" Hope whispered fearfully.

"We might have a scrap but I'll hold this place until that jasper kicks through with the thousand or know the reason why." A booming voice from the darkness intercepted Peep's negative reply. Through ears in which wild blood suddenly had set up an infernal hammering he heard and recognized that voice. It belonged to Hi Binder. And the horseman who had thundered past could have been none other than Jim Thompson.

"What—does—he—mean?" Hope essayed again in a tiny voice.

Too well Peep knew what the fellow meant. Hi Binder was going to collect the thousand dollars Tommy O'Day had lost at poker. But he dared not take the girl into his confidence—yet. Already she knew more than he had intended she should. And besides, her woman's intuition was supplying her with many details that he would have spared her.

"I don't know," he found himself lying evasively.

"Peep O'Day!" she exclaimed angrily. "You are either the biggest liar I ever knew in my life or you've—you've changed entirely since—"

He clapped a hand over her mouth. The precautionary move, rough and quick as it was, came too late.

"Who's there?" the voice of Binder bawled out of the darkness.

Chapter Thirteen

In a Strange Trap

PEEP STOOD RIGID AS STONE, straining through the darkness for a glimpse of the newcomers.

Hope sidled closer to him.

"I'm sorry I—" she whispered contritely. "I didn't mean to—"

"Who's there?" Binder's voice boomed out again. "You'd better speak up or we'll cut loose with our irons."

The first wild impulse that surged up within Peep was to call Binder—to fight it out. The big-mouthed fellow was on the Flying Spear, Peep's own ranch, a trespasser, who dared challenge him. His blood boiled. He gathered himself for a leap. In the nick of time cold reason came to temper rash judgment and stifle the crazy impulse that left him eager for combat, trembling. Save for the empty forty-five, utterly worthless now in such an emergency, he was unarmed. Much as it galled, he was forced to the bitter realization that resistance not only would be foolhardy but might result in serious injury to the girl.

He cast about wildly for some way out of the predicament, determined suddenly to bluff until they could reach the house.

"What do you jaspers want on the Flying Spear?" he demanded angrily. "This here is my place. Unless you are hunting shelter you'd better make tracks—pronto."

"Is that so?" Binder's voice came back sneeringly. "We'll see about that, too. If you're heeled, don't draw, because our chances of getting you are six to one!"

"I'm heeled all right!" Peep threw back. "And I'm warning you to go easy!"

Silence greeted the challenge, a deep, ominous silence,

filled with sinister threat. Taking advantage of it, Peep pushed Hope behind him. Finding her hand in the darkness, he pulled her forward. Without a word, he moved stealthily toward the house. Before Binder spoke they had reached the door. They entered quietly, stopped just inside while he bolted it.

"Who are they?" faltered Hope, clinging to him fearfully.

"A walloper by the name of Hi Binder and his gang," Peep returned grimly. "Where they belong and what they are doing on the Satanka range has got me guessing. But I don't cotton to their looks. And I don't calculate to have you fall into their hands if I can help it." What he did not tell her was that his greatest fear for her was inspired by the fight Jim Thompson had had with the crew outside the mystery cabin far back in the canyon.

"But won't they attack the house when they find we're in here?" she whispered fearfully. "That fellow said—"

The words died in her throat.

"Throw down your gun, you're covered!" came in a weak voice from behind them.

Startled, the two wheeled. For the first time, in their excitement, they noticed that there was a fire in the stove, which gave off a ghastly, flickering light. Now that it was too late, the real solution of the problem flashed with the rapidity of lightning through Peep's mind. After the set-to in the canyon, Jim Thompson had made for the Flying Spear. There he had taken refuge from the storm and had settled down for the night. For some reason or other, perhaps the result of the mysterious shooting at the cabin, Binder and his men had followed. Jim no doubt had heard them and given them the slip. But what Peep could not account for was the presence of one of the gang in the house.

Goaded to fury at being challenged in his own home, yet unwilling to risk drawing a shot for fear of it striking

Hope, he threw his empty forty-five to the floor. "We aren't here to start trouble," he flared hotly. "But we are here to get warm, and what's more, we're going to do it."

"Who are we?" the unseen speaker demanded.

Peep hesitated. Came to him to blurt out his own name, claim possession, and oust these trespassers. But he reasoned quickly, where the name of Tommy O'Day might possibly get by the gang, that of Peep O'Day would be a deliberate challenge. Nor would the name of Hope Thompson help. After the clash in the canyon, Binder's men would have little reason for being civil to Jim Thompson's adopted daughter. While he hated the thought of further deception, there seemed to be no other way.

"I'm Tommy O'Day," he lied, praying silently that the gloom would conceal his real identity. "I own this place. And what's more I've got a young lady with me."

"Who is she?" the voice asked.

Before Peep could answer, the girl herself spoke. "I'm Hope Thompson," she said tartly. "I'm—what right have you here? You'll pay dearly for this."

"Jim Thompson's girl?" The voice was frozen with unfriendliness.

"Yes, Jim Thompson's girl," she threw back. "And you'd better—"

"Shut up," the fellow cut her short to order roughly. "And light a lamp."

Knowing the location of the coal-oil lamp, Peep found it quickly. With no alternative, and hanging on to himself grimly, he struck a match and lighted it. Then he turned to the girl. She stood with her head thrown back defiantly, met his gaze frankly, confidingly through the flickering light. He was thankful her eyes gave no indication that she had even noticed the lie concerning his name.

With difficulty he pulled his gaze away from the picture she made with her golden hair dripping, her blue eyes sparkling with anger in the wan light. Her figure was completely covered by the bedraggled slicker. Her feet, encased in patent leather pumps, were trim and pretty in spite of the mud. He moved over to her and with gentle, almost timid hands, he drew her to a chair in front of the stove.

"I reckon you had better get those wet shoes off," he suggested solicitously. "Miss Thompson has got to dry herself and get warm before she catches cold," he told their unseen captor. "You and I are going outside."

"You may be," the fellow said sullenly, "but I ain't!"

"Gun or no gun, we're going!" Peep blazed.

There was a whine in the man's voice when he answered. "I can't. I'm shot—bad!"

Then for the first time Peep succeeded in piercing the gloom and sighting the puncher. He was stretched fully clothed on a bed which had been pushed close to the doorway of an adjoining room.

"What's the matter with you?" he demanded.

"Your damned brother shot me in Satanka!" the fellow moaned. "And Jim Thompson plugged me afterward at—"

"Jim Thompson!" Hope cried, springing to her feet. "Where is he?"

"I don't know," the cowboy growled. "But we'll find him some time. Hi—the gang—they were taking me to town to a doctor when we jumped him here at this cabin. Damn him, he gave us the slip and got away. I played out."

Peep scarcely heard the recital to an end. If the puncher spoke the truth—and there would be no reason for him lying—then he, Peep, had killed no one in the saloon brawl at Satanka.

"Was there anybody else shot in the fight in Jumbo?" Peep asked eagerly.

"Binder was winged."

"But nobody killed?"

"No. But that half-witted sheriff at Satanka thinks there was. And we're just going to let him keep on thinking it so he'll help us get our hooks on that there other O'Day walloper."

"But Jim Thompson?" Hope put in anxiously.

His own mind far easier as a result of the fellow's disclosure, Peep attempted to change the subject before the girl learned about the fight in the canyon brakes. "I reckon you'll have to let your clothes dry on you," he remarked, stirring up the fire.

"Do you suppose Jim is all right?" she persisted.

"Don't worry," he told her carelessly. "If they had harmed him this walloper would be crowin' about it."

"But I want to know!" she cried. "What has happened? What started all this trouble? What—"

"I don't know any more about it than you do," he admitted. "But why fret about it now? Forget it until we get back to the T-7. Then we can—"

The sound of heavy footsteps suddenly came from outside to cut him short.

"Unbolt that door!" ordered the man on the bed.

Peep took one look at the forty-five the fellow held braced against the pillow. With no alternative, he did what he was bid. Binder and five men sprang inside, guns drawn.

"Might as well stash 'em," Peep said, his spirits falling at the sight of the evil-faced gang, only to soar as he counted them. "I'm not even heeled." There had been six of the punchers besides Binder in the Jumbo. And now, including the wounded man on the bed, they were all here! He was not a murderer!

A lightened sense of security gave way to cold fury. But he hung onto himself grimly, kept well back in the shadows as Binder advanced.

"You're that damned Peep O'Day, ain't you?" the piggish-faced man demanded belligerently.

"No." The lie that had become so easy formed instantly on Peep's lips. "I'm Tommy O'Day."

A moment of ominous silence. Then: "You look a heap like that other," Binder countered craftily. "The one who shot my pard and me in the Jumbo, not him I was playing cards with."

"We do look a lot alike," Peep admitted, outwardly confident, but seething inside. "Folks are always getting us mixed up." He could feel the question in Hope's eyes. But he refused stubbornly to meet them. Instead he looked squarely at Binder, who, one arm in a sling—on which there was a fresh stain of blood—stood spread-legged before him. For the moment he regretted that he had not accounted for one of the evil-faced crew, gloated inwardly at the fact that, at least, they bore more scars of the Satanka combat than he did. "You ought to remember I left the Jumbo to take a young lady home," he reminded.

"Old Jim Thompson's girl!" Binder exclaimed. "Is this her?"

"It is," Hope answered before Peep could speak.

"And that's just a real streak of luck," Binder guffawed. "I reckon now we'll even things up with that—with him."

"That is where you are dead wrong," Peep said coolly. "Just because Miss Thompson and I are—We're pulling out for the T-7 with daylight."

"You just think you are!" Binder taunted.

He leered at Peep for an instant, then turned to the man on the bed. "You got his gun, didn't you?"

"It's yonder on the floor," the fellow groaned. "I was too weak—"

Binder kicked the empty forty-five into a corner and swung back to capture Peep's whipping gaze.

"That cabin deal still stands, don't it?" he shot in abruptly.

Chapter Fourteen

A Trick for a Walloper

THE POINT-BLANK QUESTION caught Peep off his guard. Yet, instinctively on the alert, he swallowed the swift denial that sprang to his lips, recognizing in the query a ruse by Binder to convince himself that he was talking to Tommy. What the deal was the fellow referred to he had no idea. But the cabin, he reasoned quickly, could be none other than the one in the canyon. This, no doubt, was the business that had demanded Tommy's attention at the Jumbo. "Sure it does," he replied carelessly, after a time.

"That's good," Binder returned, apparently satisfied. "I wasn't just plumb sure you wasn't your hell-raising brother. You look so much alike. And you ain't forgetting you owe me a thousand bucks. We'll figure the cabin in on the deal. Say for—oh, two hundred. It ain't so much. If you ain't got the other eight hundred you can just make up your mind you're going through with what we was augerin' about in town!"

The puzzled Peep heard him with uneasiness, hoping the fellow would stop talking in riddles before he was tripped up and his true identity discovered; either that, or show his hand completely. But this, apparently, Binder was too shrewd a gambler to do.

Eight hundred dollars! Peep did not believe that his father had left half that sum. But it was Binder's reference to "what we were augerin' about in town" that bothered him. He resolved to get Hope to the T-7 safely, then be free to argue with the piggish-faced man in a language he could understand.

He glanced at the dingy window. The rain had ceased. Dawn was breaking in a cold, gray chill.

"I'm not packing that much loose change," he said sarcastically. "I can raise it in Satanka. I'll saddle and hit the trail. You wait for me."

"You'd rather pay than go through with the other deal?" asked Binder, in surprise, Peep thought.

"Reckon I would," Peep answered without the slightest idea of what he was refusing to do.

"All right. Suit yourself. But don't forget—I know just plenty of things that will make it damned hard on you if—"

The unfinished warning set Peep's nerves on edge. But he dared not attempt to draw the fellow out, for fear of giving his own bluff away. So he held his tongue. After a moment the silence became strained. Turning, he strode over to where Hope huddled before the fire.

"Come on," he said. "You can ride as far as the T-7 with me, then I'll go on to Satanka and—get the—"

"Oh, no, you don't," Binder put in sneeringly. "Of course, we trust you. But we haven't got any guarantee you'll come back. The girl stays right here until you bring the money!"

"You wouldn't dare hold me!" Hope blazed, leaping to her feet to face them furiously. "Jim would run you out of the country."

"Yeah, about the same time a rabbit runs off a coyote," Binder guffawed. "This here Thompson ain't so much. And he's going to be mighty careful about who he's tackling from now on. We've got a score to settle with him. Just plenty big. And I reckon this is as good a way as any to do it."

"This deal is between you and me!" Peep said coldly. "If I go after that money she goes with me as far as the T-7. If I stay, you're out of luck all the way round, because—"

"Don't be too sure about that." An evil grin lit Binder's ugly face. "I know enough about you so you don't dare get too funny. And get this—we're planking ourselves right down in this shack until you pay up. Leave the girl here till you get the money or I'll do plenty of talking among the ranchers."

Convinced now, for some unknown reason, that Binder had been Tommy's companion that day on the range near the T-7 and was in possession of facts which his brother dared not let him reveal, Peep hesitated, casting about for some way out. Concern for Tommy gave way to fury at the threat to hold Hope, in reprisal for the debt. Yet, unarmed and overwhelmingly outnumbered, he was powerless to prevent it. He groaned inwardly at his impotence.

His glance whipped around the room, veiled in shadows that crept and danced in the wan light. Save for the firearms carried by the crew there was no weapon of any kind. Yet Binder, he noticed, had two guns stuck in his belt. One of them he recognized, by its round butt, as the forty-one he himself had dropped in the Jumbo. The other he could not see plainly because of the poor light.

"I reckon there isn't anything keeping us from getting a bite to eat," he suggested, suddenly resorting to strategy to spar for time to map out a definite course of action. "Some hot coffee will warm us all up. We'll all feel better with something under our belts."

"That's the ticket!" Binder exclaimed, wincing with pain as he suddenly shifted his bandaged arm. "Let's throw a feed into us and auger afterward."

"Sure jake with me." Peep leaned across Hope to cram wood in the stove. "Sit still," he said aloud. Then: "Use your head now like you've always used it," he whispered. "Keep your ears open. I'll give you a break pronto. Watch for it. Play it for all it's worth. Skip and ride—like hell. But once you're away, for God's sake don't mention tonight to a living soul—nobody." He kicked the red-hot door of the stove shut.

"What's that?" Binder demanded suspiciously.

"I was just telling Miss Thompson that it seems to be getting a little warmer now that our clothes are drying," Peep lied smoothly. "One of you wallopers set the table. You'll find plenty of utensils over yonder there in that drawer. Binder, you get down the bacon." He stopped short to lift his hat and scratch his head thoughtfully. "Where did we put that bacon?" he asked blankly, looking directly at Hope.

"That's what I ran into in the dark," she smiled, taking the cue with an ease that thrilled him. "Don't you remember? It's hanging outside. I know right where it is. I'll get it."

Peep felt a smug sense of satisfaction at the girl's quick wit. He had depended on her. And—she had not failed him. Before Binder could protest, she had leaped to her feet, crossed the room, and dashed outside.

Minutes passed. The silence deepened. The booted feet began to shift nervously. Binder began to grow restless. One of the gang strode to the open door.

"Don't try any funny business," Binder warned, casting a baleful glance at Peep, who stared back at him coolly.

As he spoke a thunder of hoofs arose from the barnyard. A horse went thundering and splashing away in the dim light of dawn.

"You damned cur!" Binder snarled, bolting over toward the open door, into which the others already were crowding. "You tricked us."

Peep joined them leisurely. "Tricked you?" he asked innocently. "Why, what are you talking about? I didn't think for a minute that—" He broke off.

Binder crowded to the door, leaned far out, peering into the wan light. His back was squarely toward Peep. Acting on a sudden reckless impulse, Peep reached out and seized a gun from his belt. The rounded-butt gun, his gun. Binder spun about.

"It's my turn now, jaspers," Peep taunted, leaping back

and away from the range of the man on the bed. "Unbuckle your cartridge belts, every mother's son—throw them down—and be damned quick about it."

Taken completely by surprise, the gangsters turned slowly. The blue barrel bearing down on them took reluctant fingers to belt buckles. Slowly they worked. One by one the cartridge belts, with holstered guns, dropped to the floor.

"You're Peep O'Day, not Tommy!" Binder blurted out in the light of sudden discovery. "I've been suspicious right along. And remember—no walloper ever tricked me yet and got away with it."

"Here's one jasper who did," Peep threw back tauntingly. "Keep those hands of yours dusting cobwebs off the ceiling until I get started. Because this here gun is liable to go off."

Edging past the bewildered crew, he gained the door, backed from the house. With cautious feet he found the step, the gun keeping the snarling gang still in the doorway. Then he was down—was backing through the ooze to the barn. An endless time passed. Then he backed into the barn.

Giving a last quick look, he bounded inside. Once there, he peeked through a crack. The crew was where he had left them, silhouetted against the light, hands high above their heads. A chuckle escaped him. It was answered by the soft whinny of a horse. Darting over to it, he found that its bridle still clung by the headstall. He rigged the horse up hastily, vaulted onto its back. One last look at the gang standing like statues and he crowded through the narrow door, raced for the open prairies.

A few lunges and a fusillade of shots roared out. Lead sang about his ears. But the bullets only splattered harmlessly in the mud.

Ahead he could make out Hope's horse, a dim, shapeless object, running down Surprise Creek. He roweled savagely to overtake her, but pulled rein.

"There's no use in catching up with her," he muttered to himself. "I'll trail her to the ranch to see that she gets there all right. Then I'll go on into town and square Tommy with the sheriff."

Holding a tight rein on his bit-fighting mount, he jogged along at a safe distance behind the girl, shifting sidewise in his saddle from time to time to keep an eye on the back trail. But apparently Binder and his gang gave no thought to pursuit, for he heard no hoofbeats behind.

The sky brightened. Fire yellow set the horizon to flaming. A fling of vivid color lifted on the gray flats. Peep was only half conscious of it. His eyes were on the horse and the rider ahead. A rider who strangely, he thought, never once looked back.

On the crest of a hogback he pulled rein to watch Hope ride into the T-7. When he had seen her swing down, pull the saddle from her mount, walk onto the porch, and disappear into the house, he dragged his reluctant pony about and started on toward Satanka.

Chapter Fifteen

THE TWO FORTY-ONES

THE SUN WAS SWIMMING HIGH in a sea of metal brilliance when Peep O'Day roweled his jaded pony into the deserted street of Satanka. He had traveled the long, slippery miles between the T-7 and town with scarcely a notice of time or distance. The wild running of the horse seemed to ease his violent emotions. When the brute refused to heed the stinging rowels, and slowed down of its own accord to blow, his mind began anew its mad churning.

Now he was pounding along like mad across the treacherous, muddy flats, now moving at a snail's pace. But always his thoughts were spinning like a whirligig, although his body, logy with utter weariness, moved only with effort and then seemed lifeless, something apart.

Once in Satanka, he managed to drag himself from the consuming lethargy into which he had fallen. He jerked straight in his saddle, held his shying mount under tight rein as he roweled up between the weather-beaten buildings toward the jail. Reaching it, he dismounted stiffly and tied his leg-weary pony to the fence that surrounded the 'dobe structure, with its small barred windows. His footsteps lagged as he went up the short path to the door and knocked.

When repeated knocking failed to bring any response, he tried the door. It was unlocked and yielded to his touch. He entered noisily to pause just inside and look around. But the place was deserted. Even the steel grating to the cells stood open. Satanka harbored many criminals—drifters along the owlhoot trail dodging in and out ahead of posses—but few of them ever found their way into the 'dobe jail.

Satisfied that no one was about, he threw himself wearily into a chair and cocked his muddy boots onto a table. The lazy posture was deliciously restful. He settled down comfortably to await the sheriff's return.

His cool gray eyes, bloodshot now from lack of sleep and heavy with weariness, roved idly over the dingy office. A roll-top desk in one corner was battered, covered with dust and cobwebs, piled high with papers and unopened circulars. It stood beside the door leading into the cells. The table onto which he had cocked his muddy boots was deeply scarred by careless rowels and bordered with grooves burned by forgotten cigarets. Reward notices plastered the walls, grimy with dust and age. A rifle rested across the spiked horns of a buck deer, glassy-eyed and dingy with dirt. A typical Western sheriff's office, unswept, disordered, coldly austere and uninviting.

Tiring presently of his survey, and overcome by his utter weariness, he closed his aching eyes and fell to dozing. And it was there Bud Hamby, the sheriff, found him that evening, snoring peacefully.

Hamby was typical of the men who attempted to enforce the lax law in many of the towns sprinkled through cowland. He was stubby of build and ran to paunch. His wind-whipped, corrugated face, with its double chin and pouches, was too fat to be stern. The faded blue eyes that peered out from beneath a floppy brimmed hat were more inclined to twinkle than to glint. Save for the gray in a mat of unkempt hair he might have passed for twenty for all the age his face revealed.

Bud Hamby was neither swift nor slow. Rather he was inclined to be stodgy—physically and mentally. But what he lacked in wit he made up in courage. He had yet to encounter the man who could back him down—at poker, talk, or gunplay. For the forty-five belted high on his ample thigh was by no means a show weapon. The stock of that gun was worn smooth as glass from years of constant service. The sensitive hair-trigger was of his own filing. That gun had reaped its toll of human life. And Bud Hamby still possessed the same courage that had backed his wildly reckless gunplay before age had faded his hair and slowed down the amazing speed with which that forty-five once had leaped to its holster's rim to spit death.

As a sheriff Bud Hamby was no better or no worse than scores of others in cowland. Yet he did his duty as he saw it, in a slow, methodical way, his greatest attribute a tenacity of purpose that was little short of stubbornness.

"Well, I'll be damned!" Bud exploded as he touched a match to a coal-oil lamp, which flared up to reveal the snoring Peep. "What are you doing here?"

"What did I tell you?" Before Peep, startled out of a sound sleep, could bolt upright and reply, a second man, who had entered with Hamby, moved out from the shadows. It was Tommy.

"Didn't I tell you you had the wrong jasper?" Peep's brother demanded. "But you are so damned bull-headed nobody can tell you anything. You just had to bull your way through—had to get me in bad with the whole bunch —and especially old Jim Thompson."

"Thought Jim rode up on the Belle Fourche hunting rustlers?" Peep rubbed his bloodshot eyes, dragged his feet from the table top, and stretched.

Tommy shot him an inscrutable glance, a glance that left Peep wondering.

"Jim told me in the Jumbo he was going up the river, but he came on back to the T-7 instead," Tommy said sourly. "He got there just ahead of Hope, who traipsed in sometime after daybreak. She closed up like a clam and wouldn't tell anybody where she had been. That r'iled old Jim terrible and he raised particular hell about it."

Tommy shifted nervously under Peep's gaze.

"You see—that team of broncs ran away last night in the storm," he offered apologetically. "Throwed Hope out of the buckboard. I got 'em stopped about a quarter of a mile down the road and drove back. But it was so dark and—I never laid eyes on her again. I hunted all over hell's half acre for her. Couldn't find her. Figuring she was all right and had lit out, I went to the T-7. I only got in a little while ahead of her this morning. She came from somewhere on horseback. Old Jim was as sore as a crippled coyote."

Peep got lazily to his feet, yawned, moved about stiffly, and recaptured his brother's roving gaze.

"Well?"

"Bud here loped in to the ranch with a posse. He'd been to the Flying Spear. There wasn't anybody there so he makes tracks on to the T-7. I got there just a little before he did. He was all het up and figuring to arrest somebody. I tried my dangdest to tell him I was Tommy. But he got me in bad by saying I was you, or you was me, or—and I couldn't explain to the mullet-headed old fossil. He arrested me for murder—thanks to you—my brother."

"You can go now." Peep was conscious of an inward cringing at the sting in Tommy's last words, yet singularly elated with the knowledge that for all Thompson's anger Hope had revealed nothing of their escapade.

"Go on back to the T-7 and square yourself with old Jim. Tell him I lied about the names—that I'm responsible for everything—and you weren't to blame." He swung on Hamby, who for all his silence was watching him with hawklike intensity. "He's telling you straight, Bud. He's Tommy. I'm Peep. I did that shooting in the Jumbo. I'm the man you want."

The sheriff lifted his sodden hat to run gnarled fingers through the mat of gray hair and push it back from his corrugated brow. "I know it now," he growled after he had surveyed the two carefully. "Since I can see the both of you together. So it was you who did the shooting at the Jumbo?"

"Reckon it was," Peep admitted in a hollow voice.

"See," Tommy blurted out angrily. "And you got me in bad with Hope and all the rest of them—I tried to tell you. But you bull-headed old— Jim is looking for a new foreman," he told Peep almost gloatingly. "He told me to tell you, if I saw you, that he wouldn't have any jasper around the T-7 who couldn't stay out of saloon brawls. What did you want to butt in and start that row for?"

Peep's teeth clicked grimly. Old Jim was looking for a new foreman to replace him after he had worked so hard for the job! But the thing passed quickly, forgotten in a surge of anger at Tommy's obvious attempt to shift all the blame for the Jumbo affair.

"You know why I did it," he flared back bitterly, so bitterly that Tommy winced and stepped back. "But nobody else will ever know. Unless you tell 'em. It's between you and me. Now you shag it on down to the ranch and make peace. Just a minute—" as Tommy, plainly anxious to be gone, turned toward the door. "That money you lost—I'll get it some way and we'll pay Binder. I'm telling you—don't let that fourflusher get anything on you."

Tommy flushed guiltily, but held his tongue.

Hamby snorted with impatience. "Cut out the rag-chewing and get the hell out of here so I can sleep," he exploded. "I'm sorry I arrested you, but a sheriff can't be expected to know the difference between—between two peas."

"That's all right now." The careless laugh Tommy essayed was high-pitched and nervous. "I'm going—and damned willingly. I'm sure glad I'm not in Peep's boots. So-long."

The door slammed behind him. Peep stood transfixed, his face white with anger, lips set in a thin grim line across his teeth. Hamby interrupted his bitter retrospection. He moved heavily to the chair, dropped into it.

"Well, what did you do it for?" he demanded gruffly.

"Do what?" Peep swung around to eye him coldly.

"Kill that walloper at the Jumbo."

"What walloper?"

"Why that—that jasper at the Jumbo." Hamby's heavy voice trembled with subdued rage.

"Is he dead?"

"Sure he is dead. That is—leastwise he was dying when I left town trailing you in that damned storm. Doc said he wouldn't live an hour. You'll pay plenty for this."

"Even Doc can go wrong, can't he?" Peep again was master of his riotous emotions, the cold-as-steel Peep with glittering eyes and a confidence that broke down the nerve of other men.

"What do you mean?" Hamby's tone was sneering.

"Just what I said," Peep shot back. "And you don't need to get so tough with your tones either. That jasper I shot in the Jumbo isn't dead, no matter what Doc or anybody else says."

"He is! Doc said—"

"I don't give a damn what Doc said. I talked with that walloper this morning."

Hamby came heavily to his feet. "What?"

"I'm telling you."

"Where was he?"

"At the Flying Spear."

"The Flying Spear?" The sheriff's jaw sagged with amazement. "I didn't nose around none after I rode in with—with Tommy," he admitted sheepishly. "I come right up here. I was so danged tired and— But that jasper was dying when I left town."

"Mebbeso," Peep snorted. "But he didn't die."

"What did you come back here for if you knew he was alive?" The slow-thinking Hamby could not conceal his unbelief.

"Because I told you at the Jumbo I'd be back. I always try to keep my word."

"Yeah." Hamby's darting glance was indicative of his slow-moving thoughts. "You might be telling me straight," he reasoned craftily. "And then again you might not. I'll just lock you up and go talk to the coroner. Pass over that Colt you're toting."

Without protest Peep drew the gun he had snatched from Binder's belt at the Flying Spear.

"I'm only doing this because I want to work with you on the case," he said coldly. "Not because you or anybody else can take my gun. I want you to know that, Hamby. But there's a lot of things— Take care of it. It was Paw's gun. I wouldn't have anything happen to it for the world."

Extending the gun, butt first, Peep looked at it again to satisfy himself that he had read the initials aright in the Jumbo. Those initials seemed to have a singular, impelling attraction. But now his glance became a fixed, wide-eyed stare. Instead of the *J.T.* he had expected, the initials *H.O.* were burned into the bull's-eye on the stock. Hank O'Day—his father. He recovered quickly and set to reasoning. He had lost a gun with the initials J.T. in the Jumbo. He had seen it in Binder's belt; he knew he would know it anywhere because of its odd caliber, its rounded butt. He had snatched the gun, only to find now that the initials were H.O.

His thoughts raced like lightning, cascaded through his mind. His father had told him that the son of a man he had killed was in possession of his gun. That gun had been in the possession of— There was but one conclusion to draw. Hi Binder and not Jim Thompson, as he had come to suspect, was the son of the man old Hank had killed. But the initials J.T., on the butt of the other forty-one, what connection did they have with Hi Binder? Who was this Binder anyway? Was he traveling under an alias? In reality were his initials J.T.—the same as those of Jim Thompson?

More perplexed than ever before in his life, he slowly passed the gun over to the waiting Hamby, who seized it to examine it curiously.

"A forty-one Colt," the sheriff mused aloud. "I never saw one before in this country. Funny-looking, ain't it, with a round butt!"

"Look at the initials." For no particular reason he could think of at the moment, Peep pointed them out in the bull's-eye on the stock.

"H.O." Hamby observed slowly. "Hank O'Day's gun. I recklect of him always toting it now, although I don't know of him ever drawing it on a human. It sure hadn't ought to be very hard to connect you up with this shooting, had it?"

"Easiest thing in the world," Peep returned carelessly. "Even you could connect me up with it—provided, of course, that there was a man killed. But you'd better find out before you go to—"

"Don't think I'm not going to." Striding across the room, Hamby locked the forty-one carefully in his battered desk. Then he came back to where Peep stood to search him for more weapons. "I reckon we'll be able to find plenty against you."

Peep only shrugged. Nor did he offer any protest as Hamby jerked a thumb toward the door. He entered without a word. When he was inside, Hamby turned the key in the lock. Then he busied himself about the musty office for a time, turned down the coal-oil lamp, and went out. Peep stared after him thoughtfully. Presently he threw himself on a cot in one of the cells and set about trying to solve the mystery of the two forty-one guns.

Chapter Sixteen

UNEXPECTED WEALTH

HOURS LATER, according to Peep's way of thinking, Hamby returned. For an endless period of time he had paced the single corridor between the four steel cells in an agony of torment. Now he was thinking of Tommy, of the hair rope with the streak of yellow in it. Now his riotous thoughts had sped on to Binder and his gang as he had last seen them, standing like statues framed in the light of the Flying Spear door. He wondered.

His thoughts swept on to Hope. He had seen her ride into the T-7, dismount, and enter the house. But Tommy had said Old Jim had been— Old Jim, who was supposed to be somewhere up the Belle Fourche, but who had bobbed up—from nowhere—in the canyon to— It was all a maze—a baffling, churning problem.

The return of Hamby interrupted his meditation. The sheriff came stamping in to bang the door behind him. Peep saw him turn up the light. After a careful survey of the interior of the cells, he started pacing restlessly about the office.

"Well, what is it? Murder?" Peep walked over to the grated door to ask quietly after a time.

Hamby halted abruptly and whirled. "I don't know," he snapped.

"Is anybody dead?"

"I don't know that either."

"Well, what does that make me?" Peep demanded bitingly. "What are you going to do with me? I don't know much about law. But it seems to me that in a case of murder the law has got to produce the body—and that if it comes to a straight shooting affair there has to be a complaining witness."

"I can hold you on a disturbance charge because I happen to have been a witness to that fracas," Hamby snarled.
"So don't get too damned cocky. I'd like to give you life
for raising hell—for making me spend the night hunting
you in that storm. But I can't find any corpse."

"Didn't I tell you I talked with the jasper I shot this
morning?"

"That's what you said. But wallopers in jail aren't not-
ed for telling the truth. There are some other angles to
this thing too—that you don't know about. A couple of
jaspers kidnaped Doc this afternoon. Blindfolded him
and took him out to a cabin on horseback. Doc can't tell
for the life of him what direction he went even. But he
swears he never was in that cabin before. Once they had
him inside they peeled the blindfold. But they'd hung
blankets on the walls so he couldn't recognize a picture
or a scantling or anything if he saw it again."

"But what the devil did they want to kidnap Doc for?"
Peep demanded blandly.

"There was a fellow in that cabin shot bad. Dying.
Doc done what he could for him. But he says the jig is
up, that the fellow won't live the night out. When Doc
had finished treating the wounded jasper, they paid him
off, blindfolded him again, and brought him back to
town." Hamby strode over to the grating and stood
spread-legged, thumbs hooked in his cartridge belt, glaring through the flickering shadows at Peep. "Doc will
swear that dying man he worked on today is the same
jasper he fixed up after the shooting in the Jumbo last
night. The man you shot. What do you think of that?"

Peep started violently in spite of himself. The same
man! Yet—a mental picture of the cabin in the canyon
as he had seen it the night before flashed into his mind.
It was on the tip of his tongue to reveal the whole affair
and to lead Hamby to this newly constructed mystery

abode. But, suddenly determined to run down the mystery of the thing alone, he let it pass.

"What are you going to do with me?" he found himself asking, after a time.

"That's just the problem," Hamby admitted sourly. "While he was tending to that fellow, Doc took a bullet out of him. It was a forty-one. Near as we can figure, it was identical with the one Doc cut out of the same jasper last night. That proves a hell of a lot. Proves that you did the shooting because you are packing the only forty-one I ever heard of on this range or any other."

Came to Peep another notion to blurt out the whole truth, to reveal that there was another forty-one on the Satanka range. But not knowing to whom it belonged, he remained silent.

"Doc sure must of been crazy last night," he observed scornfully.

"How is that?" Hamby demanded sourly.

"Why didn't he take the two forty-one bullets out of the jasper when he was first tending to him?"

"Well—" Hamby swelled up angrily. "Because there wasn't two in him, that's why. He cut one out."

"And after I'd shot him once, I supposed I followed him all night through that storm to shoot him again?" Peep smiled wanly. "That will sound plausible in court, won't it, Hamby? Especially in view of the fact that you and a posse were crowding right along on my heels all night. You'd better guess again."

As Peep argued the thing aloud, his thoughts were taking a more definite shape in his mind. The wounded man at the Flying Spear had admitted to him that both he—Peep—and Jim Thompson had shot him. But how, if Thompson had fired the second bullet into the fellow, had it been with a forty-one caliber when he had dropped one in the Jumbo, and had taken its mate from Binder—probably the only forty-ones ever seen on the Satanka range? The more he tried to straighten the thing out in his mind the more involved it seemed to become.

"You haven't answered my question yet," he reminded him, plainly enjoying Hamby's ill-concealed perplexity. "There is a man dying from a forty-one bullet wound. You claim I am toting the only forty-one in the country. And I am ready to plead guilty to the Jumbo shooting. Just how does the law read in a case like that?"

Hamby paced about angrily for a moment, his heels banging the floor, rowels jangling. Then without so much as a word, he re-crossed to the door, unlocked it and jerked it wide.

"The law is plain providing we have the wounded man, or a corpse, or some kind of proof," he growled. "But we haven't. That fellow was sure a good imitation of a dying man last night. Doc came to the Jumbo right behind me to see what the racket was about just as you flew the coop. He fixed up one fellow's arm and had the bad-shot jasper carried to his office. I was so all-fired sore I didn't wait to see what happened. I rounded up the boys and lit out after you.

"Doc tells me he cut a forty-one out of that jasper. His pards asked as long as he was dying if they couldn't move him to the hotel. Doc, the danged fool, let 'em. That's the last he ever seen of that dying man until he treated him for a new bullet wound out in a cabin somewheres today—and took another forty-one slug out of him, which he claims wasn't there after the saloon ruckus."

Peep's wan smile angered the boiling sheriff.

"It's a plain case of murder, that's what it is," Hamby bellowed. "With the fellow who admits the shooting in jail and no corpse, nor nothing, to prove it with. The county attorney is getting gray-headed and drunker than a hoot owl every minute trying to figure it out. What's a jasper to do? I can't hold you for murder until he's sobered up enough to get out the warrant. I might lay an assault with a deadly weapon charge against you—"

"On whose complaint?" Peep asked mildly.

"My own if I feel like it," Hamby roared. "Or mebbeso the law might dig up a John Doe or something. Besides, there's always a disturbance charge. We've got plenty against you, young fellow. So don't get too all-fired cocky. Now you take a sneak before I get r'iled up again and lock you up for keeps."

"Am I free?"

"I'm not saying we won't pick you up again pronto, by a long ways," Hamby hedged. "And I'm warning you not to try to get out of the country. 'Cause I'll ride you down if—"

Peep's answer was to stride across the office, jerk open the door, and slam it behind him. His pony, still slumped wearily where he had left it tied to the fence, whinnied softly. Securing the reins, he swung up and rode down the street.

A short distance and he drew rein, undecided what course to pursue. He rebelled at the idea of returning to the T-7 at the present time. He could go down to the Flying Spear. Yet, with the sudden thought of the thousand dollars Tommy had lost—of Hi Binder—of his pledge to raise the money—it drove all else from his mind.

Late as it was, a feeble light still came from the Bank of Satanka. Roweling across the street, he dismounted and peered into the window. The cashier and two men, whom Peep did not know but took by their clothes for commission men—there are always commission men in cowtowns —were engaged in conversation. He tapped on the pane. Recognizing him, the cashier came to the front door and let him in. Then, with a muttered excuse, he left Peep and returned to the strangers to pick up the conversation in lowered tones.

Peep idled about. Guarded mention of the name of Jim Thompson caused him to prick up his ears. He strained to catch what the three were saying.

"He hasn't even paid the interest on that five thousand mortgage," came to him in little more than a whisper. "He's got to do something. He just shipped two thousand head, which will clean up part of his indebtedness. Is there any way of finding out how many more cattle he can let go?"

"That's his foreman there now, I believe." The cashier smiled and nodded toward Peep. "You're Peep, aren't you?"

"Yes." Peep strode forward toward the trio, which sized him up in a single glance.

"How many head of cattle can Jim Thompson gather after just shipping?" the cashier asked. "By that we don't mean she-stuff that will drain his herd, but young stuff, feeders—"

"Offhand I'd say in the neighborhood of a thousand head," Peep answered thoughtfully. "But there would be barren she-stuff in that."

"Thanks." Apparently dismissed by the abrupt word from one of the commission men, Peep resumed his idle waiting while the three went back to their guarded undertones.

"A thousand head, including barren she-stuff, won't do it," drifted to him. "The stuff he has shipped will probably take care of his past-due paper. But there is five thousand more due in thirty days. We're tired of carrying him. We'll wait the month; then, unless he can pay that five thousand, we have no choice. We'll foreclose."

The trio arose presently and moved toward the door. Peep stared after them, pondering what he had overheard. Old Jim Thompson had admitted to him that his finances were not in the best of shape, but he had not intimated that things were so serious as this. Foreclosure on the T-7— The closing of the door and the return of the cashier interrupted his thoughts.

"I've been waiting for you to come in, Peep," the banker said pleasantly. "Your father had a world of confidence in you. Before he died we had a long talk. It seems as though he was afraid your brother would be reckless if he got hold of the money he left. He told me not to let Tommy have it, or any part of it, unless you were with him."

"I'm not wanting any of the money for myself now," Peep explained. "But Tommy—well, the kid kind of got into a jackpot and he is needing a thousand bucks right bad. I don't reckon Paw left that much but—I thought mebbeso there might be some way we could mortgage the Spear and—"

The cashier laughed. "Didn't Hank ever tell you what he was worth?"

"Paw never told anybody anything. But he didn't leave any thousand dollars, I'm betting."

"He left several times a thousand. His account is something over twelve thousand dollars. I can't give you the exact figures tonight as all our books are in the vault, but if you'll come in tomorrow I'll have them for you."

"Twelve thousand dollars!" Peep gasped incredulously. "Why—that's a hell of a pile of money! I'm going on to the ranch tonight and I don't suppose I'll be able to get back tomorrow. There isn't a way— Could you fix me up so I could get hold of a thousand of it if I needed it in a hurry before I can get back to town."

"Sure." Going behind the grating, the cashier tossed over a checkbook and a signature card. "Just sign your name there for our files," he requested, turning up the coal-oil wall-bracket light. "Take the checkbook along with you. We'll honor your check for any amount up to— say, six thousand. Then come in as quickly as you can and we'll get the whole thing straightened out and decide how you want it handled."

Thanking him, and tucking the checkbook safely beneath his chaps, Peep left the bank, his mind in a whirl.

Yet once again in the saddle, and heading toward the Jumbo for a bite of food, the knowledge that he was the possessor of so much money did not lessen the heaviness that had settled down upon him. In a few short hours he had sunk from a man respected to a jobless drifter under the sharp eye of the law. Even old Jim Thompson, whom he had supposed his staunchest friend, had turned against him.

"I reckon there are other places on earth besides this Satanka range," he mused aloud, roweling his jaded pony up to the hitch rack and swinging down stiffly. "We'll throw a feed under our belt, lope on out to the T-7, catch up Torpedo, and give you a rest, horse. Then I'll jog on up yonder in the canyon and pay Mister Binder a visit." Scarcely knowing it, his rowels bit into the animal. It lunged ahead. "And on that visit I reckon Mister Hi Binder will do some talking. Fact is, he'll spill his guts, or—"

Making fast the horse, which immediately dropped its weight on three legs to doze, he entered the Jumbo, which was deserted, and strode noisily to the lunch counter.

A half-hour later he drained his second cup of coffee, paid for the meal, and went outside, feeling better with a full stomach. Mounting, he headed into the night for the T-7.

Chapter Seventeen

A BAFFLING MYSTERY

THROUGH INDETERMINABLE HOURS, Peep roweled his weary mount across the prairies. Patches of gumbo and alkali, still slippery from the rain, made treacherous the gloomy wastes. The darkness, which hung like an enveloping mantle over the flats, slowed his pace. The only light came from the stars, flung like a spangled banner in a Stygian sea. The stillness of the region was as vast and awesome as the darkness itself, unbroken save for the thin whispers of night life that seemed shrill, beating on eardrums tuned to every sound.

Eyes aching, body hunched with fatigue, his bones like tallow, Peep pushed on. When finally he climbed down at the gate of the T-7, his legs were so leaden with weariness they would scarcely support his weight. Several times during the dark and dreary ride from town he had fallen asleep, while his pony, almost as weary as himself, had plodded along gamely.

Dropping the gate, he led the animal through, replaced it, and instead of trying again to mount, led the brute toward the barn. The big ranch was in utter darkness, even the bunkhouses, the punchers long since having snuffed out the lanterns and rolled in.

Going directly to the corral, he located Torpedo. Dragging the saddle off the brute he had ridden from town, and turning it into the home pasture, where it immediately took to rolling with keen delight, he returned and tossed the saddle onto the back of the snorting Torpedo. Leading the animal outside, with as little noise as possible, he mounted and pushed on in the direction of the Flying Spear.

Ahead now lay a new void of blackness, the crisscrossed cow-trails but dim yellow threads in the gloom. Stars still spangled the sky, their wan light causing the sage and greasewood to rise up about him like creatures of a hideous nightmare, distorted, misshapen. The night was filled with sound yet was vastly, awesomely quiet. The thin chirp of a cricket, the croak of a bullfrog, the whir of a startled covey of grouse, disturbed as he rode past. A cottontail, darting from beneath his pony's hoofs, startled Torpedo into shying violently. But the voice of the man on his back restored his confidence instantly. Deep down in the brakes a steer was bellowing a challenge into the night. Far ahead came back an answer, a measured lowing that wavered and fell, finally became a throb that beat on straining eardrums long after the echo had died in the distance.

Peep covered the few miles to the Flying Spear scarcely noticing. Reaching the place and finding it in darkness and unoccupied, he was tempted for a moment to remain and rest. His body was numb with weariness, his aching muscles rebelled at further punishment. The chill and damp of the night spent in the rain had seeped to the core, left him now hot, now cold. But he clicked grim teeth on the pleading of his body. Some persistent urge kept him traveling on. He reined the reluctant Torpedo on past the Flying Spear and headed toward the cabin in the canyon.

After a considerable time, guided only by instinct—a rangeman's knowledge of distances and direction which seldom is wrong—he finally rode into the rimrock above the canyon. Near the spot where he believed he had marked the trail, he dismounted, ground-picketed the fiery Torpedo, and prowled about. Although his eyes had become somewhat accustomed to the darkness, in the rimrock the gloom seemed to deepen. Yet for all of it, he presently located the stones he had piled in the rain. Going back to Torpedo, he led the unwilling, snorting brute to the trail, swung into the saddle, and started the steep descent.

Once Torpedo had negotiated the hazardous side, and had straightened out on the canyon floor, Peep moved him forward at a better pace, eyes and ears alert to the first suspicious sign. But he heard nothing, saw nothing. The cabin itself was in utter darkness. The vast solitude of chambers of the dead pervaded the place. The shrill cry of a phoebe bird, winging through limitless space above, was the only sound.

Leaving Torpedo back at a safe distance, he moved ahead stealthily. Gaining the cabin, he flattened himself against the wall and worked his way around it. At the farther end his fingers came in contact with what seemed to be a shutter. He maneuvered cautiously until he could press his ear tightly against it. His nerves went taut, seemed to sing with that tautness. While not a ray of light escaped from within, he now could catch distinctly the sound of voices raised in anger. He strained against the rough boards, listening. His heart pounded against his ribs, the louder as he tried to subdue his breathing.

"It ought to be as simple as falling off of a log," came a voice, Binder's voice. "You already own half of the Flying Spear. Noise it around that I have leased your brother's half interest. That and this cabin you fixed me up with will just about square us on that thousand-dollar debt."

Instinctively the nerve-tight Peep knew the unseen speaker who would answer.

"This cabin belongs to Jim Thompson." It was Tommy's voice, high-pitched, nervous. "I didn't have any right to let you in here in the first place. But how did I know you and Jim would tangle? Give me a little time. My God, I—I tell you I can raise that money."

"Time nothing," Binder snorted angrily. "I've already given you all the time you're going to get. You'll fork over that money right here and now or you'll play the game the way I deal—and like it. To hell with Thompson! He don't look tough to me. And besides, I've got him where he can't open his chops. Outfiguring that smart-aleck brother of yours is the easiest thing I know. I'll lease his share and we'll start stocking up."

The now thoroughly puzzled Peep had no time to wonder what Binder was driving at before Tommy spoke.

"You don't know Peep. He'll raise the devil when he finds out about—all this."

"How is he going to find out in jail?" Binder sneered. "And suppose he does find out. Just what in the devil can he do about it? It's a dead mortal cinch he's in no position to get very tough. But what if he did? I haven't seen anybody leaving the country on account of him. The best he could do would be to send the sheriff down. And you could talk him out of it. There's a hundred ways to kill a coyote if you're good—and not yellow."

"But supposing they turn Peep loose?" Tommy's voice was husky with fear.

"How the hell are they going to turn him loose?" Binder bawled furiously. "The jasper he shot is dying, isn't he? Doc says he can't live. They'll hang this fourflusher brother of yours for it sure. It's a cut-and-dried case, premeditated murder. That walloper came into the Jumbo with blood in his eye and snorting for trouble. And he got it. Even if they don't hang him they'll keep him in jail until court time. He can't even get bail on a murder charge in Wyoming."

Binder's disclosure confirmed the suspicion that suddenly had flashed into the mind of the listening Peep. It was to this cabin in the canyon that the doctor, kidnaped from Satanka, had been brought to minister to a dying man.

He waited breathlessly for Tommy's next words, which voiced a question running through his brain.

"But the fellow Peep shot isn't dead yet? How are you

going to have Peep held for murder? You said yourself that the sheriff didn't know where you brought the wounded—"

"That jasper is so near dead it wouldn't take anything to—it would be a mercy to—" Binder leered significantly. "And it's a mighty short trip to get his body back into Satanka and leave it in an alley somewheres under cover of dark. Nobody knows where we— I reckon if anything like that happened that damned brother of yours would be framed proper, wouldn't he?"

Peep heard a chair bang to the floor. "Do you mean you would kill that wounded man just to—" Tommy's voice rose wildly.

Peep strained for Binder's answer. It came—a guffaw loud, brutal, heartless.

"Well, I'll be damned if I'll be a party to it." Even as Tommy shouted his refusal Peep could sense the lack of determination behind it.

"All right, then." It was Binder again, his tone suddenly frozen, deadly. "I'll just collect the thousand you owe me some other way. And not only that, but I'll fix that brother of yours so he'll hang to boot. Damn you! You're yaller clean through, that's what you are. And him too. I'll take a lease on that Flying Spear and make you like it. I'll run things to suit myself. I'm giving you fair warning you've tried to double-cross the wrong jasper. And no matter what happens, you'd better keep your yawp shut or you'll be dangling from a cottonwood, buzzard bait yourself."

"I'm only trying to get around Peep." Tommy's voice was hoarse. "He'd never stand for it. I'm telling you you're figuring wrong. You don't know Peep."

"Don't know him? Damn him, I know all I want to about him. He won't stand for it, huh?" Binder was snarling. "He's got to stand for it. Just the same as if he was hog-tied. And like it."

"But supposing they turn him loose before—" It was

apparent that Tommy was wavering. "Before we—" he offered weakly.

"They won't," Binder said with assurance. "I'm not all damned fool. Do I lease his interest or take over yours—for good?"

"His, I guess," Tommy agreed wearily. "But I'm not going to have any hand in croaking that fellow Peep shot."

"Leave that to me." Binder laughed brutally. "You understand what you're to do?"

"Yes. But I sure hate to—"

"Listen, you yaller-bellied skunk. I won't have anybody around me with cold feet. You'll do as I say or—"

"I haven't got cold feet," Tommy cried with a flash of spirit. "And I'll tell you right now if you didn't have the goods on me you'd never get me tangled up in your dirty underhanded—nor in any scheme like this—you nor nobody else."

"Get a dally on your tongue, before I tromp all the hell out of you," Binder roared. "You haven't got any put-in, one way or another. I'm the big mogul in this deal, and all the rest of them as far as you're concerned. So get that straight—and quick!" Peep jerked straight, muscles taut, bulging. He could picture the piggish-faced man towering above the cowering Tommy, obviously browbeating him into submission. "You're only one of the gang as far as that goes." Binder was threatening again loudly, boastfully. "So remember where you belong. Now you get the hell out of here. Make tracks for the T-7 while you're all whole. And you're doing what I say, or—"

The thundering tone, Tommy's flash of half-hearted resistance, his obvious reluctance to join in with Binder's scheme, spurred Peep to action. A wild and reckless impulse seized him, took complete possession of him before he could stifle it with cold reason. He would force his way into the cabin, call Binder to account here and now. That the piggish-faced man had his gang with him mattered not. If there was one iota of fear in Peep O'Day, no man had yet discovered it. Gang or no gang, he was going in.

Before he realized it, he was moving stealthily to the door. His hand crept to the holster at his hip. He stopped short. That holster was empty. He was without firearms of any sort. The forty-one, with the initials *H.O.* burned in the bull's-eye on the rounded butt, was in the sheriff's desk back at Satanka.

He was forced to heed the dictates of reason. Much as it galled, he had no alternative but to wait. To rush head-long into the gang without a weapon was nothing short of suicide. He would learn nothing. To waylay Tommy on the trail would avail him little more. His brother would only refuse to talk, cover up with sullenness. Besides, to show himself at a time when Binder thought him safe in jail at Satanka might wreck his hope of getting to the bottom of the whole affair, which suddenly had assumed the proportion of a baffling and intriguing mystery.

Chapter Eighteen

A Stunning Discovery

BARELY CONSCIOUS OF WHAT HE WAS ABOUT, Peep moved quietly away from the door. Once again in the shadows that enshrouded the cabin, he halted, waiting. The loud voices had ceased. Silence reigned within, a silence that seemed tangible, clutched at his heart, a silence that was sinister, deadly, filled with ominous portent.

Then a movement inside broke the tension that had descended upon him. A shuffling of feet, the whine of spinning rowels. The door opened a crack to stab the gloom with a beam of light. A man squeezed through. Framed for an instant in the streak of light that leaped far out across the canyon, Peep recognized him. It was Tommy leaving the mysterious cabin—without a word—with only the utter silence of hate and ill wishes behind him.

He heard his brother swing into the saddle with a muttered curse, bring a grunt from his horse with the rowels, and dash savagely away into the night. He waited for a time, straining for any conversation that might pass between those left in the cabin. But apparently Binder had done his talking for Tommy's ears alone. For absolute silence fell after the youth had ridden away.

Disgusted, Peep stole around the cabin and started back to where he had left Torpedo. He cursed his luck as the brute whickered at his approach. But apparently the sound, if it was noticed at all, was set down for that of a prowling range animal. Getting to Torpedo's head with difficulty, he gathered up the reins, swung into the saddle, and rode away from the cabin. A rider who usually spared his mount, especially on a climb, for once Peep O'Day forgot. He goaded Torpedo to his limit up the steep trail, never once allowing the blowing brute to pause. But if the animal weakened, he gave no sign, although the wind rasped croupily in his throat.

The tedious climb ended, he put the horse through the rimrock at breakneck speed. The gigantic shadows raced past. But he paid no heed. He was bound for the Flying Spear. Presently he had dropped down through the wild brakes and had straightened the brute out on a trail toward his own ranch. The horse ran through the night like a frightened doe, head on a level with its withers, ears plastered, tail straight out like a rudder behind. The graceful floating motion that thrilled Peep now was evident. Torpedo, the ex-outlaw, the man-killer, pushed miles behind its long swinging lope with an amazing ease. And the farther the brute ran the easier came his wind. Sweat started on his ears, trickled down from the brow band. Lather foamed up beneath the cheek bands. Lather gathered at the rim of the saddle blanket and ran in rivulets across sweating flanks. But once he had caught his second wind, the animal had hit its stride—the endless stride that Peep O'Day knew would continue until the steel-hearted brute dropped in its tracks.

Presently the huddled buildings of the Flying Spear loomed up, stark and grotesque, before him. But still there was no light. Somehow the fact gave him an added sense of security. Of a sudden he was again conscious of his utter weariness; he was wilting in his saddle. It seemed that he could not go on, that all the punishment he had endured had centered in one terrible, enervating moment.

At the barn Torpedo stopped of his own accord. The half-dead Peep could feel the brute's inquisitive nose at his boot—an invitation to get off. Then he was climbing down, stiffly, scarcely realizing what he was doing. He barely remembered jerking the saddle off the animal, filling its manger, and tying it in the barn. He reeled drunkenly up the short trail toward the house, entered. He struck a match only to be sure the place was unoccupied. Then he staggered to the bunk, threw himself full length upon it, and was quickly overwhelmed with a black blanket of oblivion.

Nor did he move until late afternoon of the following day. When finally he did open his eyes, a blazing sun was laying lacy patterns across the dusty, rough board floor. Greatly refreshed, he stretched contentedly and rolled out. Hunger assailed him, hunger that left him weak and faint. Going to the pump, he stripped and took an ice cold shower. Then changing his clothes, he felt like a new man.

Returning to the house, he kindled a fire. While his bacon was frying he dragged on his chaps and went to the barn. After a careful rubdown of Torpedo—who greeted him with a whicker—he fed the brute a measure of grain. Then he went back to the house to eat ravenously, wolfing his food. The meal finished, he twisted a cigaret and idled about for a time, trying to make up his mind what to do. An hour, two hours passed. The sun sank lower on its downward course. Deep purple began to trace lines between the sage. The horizon was afire, dazzling, dancing, unreal, ever changing.

Near sundown Peep quit the house and strode out to the barn. Torpedo too now seemed anxious to be on the move, plainly relished the saddle as it crossed his back. He waited with bloated belly for the latigo to grow taut.

Then they were outside.

Outlaws! The word suddenly sprang to Peep's mind, struck him with a sinister and hidden meaning. Outlaws! Torpedo, the man-killer. Peep O'Day, the man-killer.

He stopped stock-still, found the brute's silky jaw with his fingers. It nuzzled forward. He rubbed its brow, brushed the mane back from square, pleading eyes.

"It's a hell of a world, fellow," he muttered, something of a catch in his voice. "You were a man-killer—I tamed you. You came back, found a friend. Me—I'm a man-killer too. I wonder if I'll make the same comeback—"

Torpedo's answer was to nuzzle farther forward. The brute's eyes were wide, pleading. It whickered softly. "Well, at least I've got one friend," Peep gulped. He caught himself up sharply, jerked straight. Peep O'Day giving vent to his pent-up emotions—Peep O'Day the man who looked death in the eye without flinching—Peep O'Day, the man whom all Satanka feared—with the possible exception of Hi Binder.

Peep led Torpedo to the water trough, then snapped into the saddle. There he sat for a moment, thinking. While he had no definite plan, he felt that things had now reached a point where he must take someone into his confidence, seek advice. Unarmed, he dared not return to the cabin in the canyon. He was no longer welcome at the T-7. To confide in Hamby was to— Tommy—there never had been any confidences between him and his brother. Old Jim Thompson. There was a time—but now— Hope!

Thought of the girl brought a leaden weight to his heart. Hope—he had loved her ever since he could remember. She, of all others, might at one time have understood. If he could talk to her, he was ready to explain now. She had always offered such excellent advice. Even now, he knew she would understand.

Almost before he realized it he had whirled Torpedo and was thundering away toward the T-7.

At the T-7 he would meet Tommy. His teeth clicked grimly on the thought. Tommy—his brother. He could force from Tommy a confession. And perhaps force a showdown—or he might settle the score— Or he might give Tommy the thousand dollars—might even manage a way to call Binder's hand and pay him the thousand himself.

He crossed Surprise Creek below the Ragged Hound corrals. Sight of them brought back vividly the memory of the day that old Hank had tried to ride the horse that now galloped so evenly beneath him. Brought back the day that he himself had mastered the brute. Torpedo had been bested. An outlaw spirit had been broken. He wondered at it. Wondered if his own spirit, that surged so wildly within him sometimes, would be broken too. Somehow he connected Tommy with that breaking. Outlaws—

Save for a small herd of cattle and calves working its way up the valley toward him in the cool of evening, and a bunch of horses grazing on a distant table, the flats were deserted. He pulled rein, jogged along, his riotous thoughts easing with the slower pace.

Of a sudden he jerked up, snapped taut in his saddle, sniffing the air. He had caught a whiff of smoke, the dread of rangeland. His keen sense of smell told him the smoke was from a chip fire. His gaze whipped over the region, purple in the fading light of closing day. He saw no smoke, nothing but heat shimmering upward in waves. Yet there is no fooling a cowman on that dread odor. The slow breeze that swayed the parched grass was drifting toward him from the T-7. He lifted Torpedo with his rowels.

A short distance below and he put Torpedo down the steep side of a wash, hit the bottom in a cloud of dust and flying chunks of gumbo. He rode into a small bunch of cattle. The brutes stopped grazing, to look in terror for a moment then take to their heels, to run in half circles and stare back at him. The she-stuff bawled raucously for the calves that clung awkwardly to their sides. Peep reined Torpedo to a walk. With the practiced eye of a cowman, he read the brands of the lumbering brutes.

"Well, I'll be damned!" escaped lips that were suddenly braced in a thin grim line across set teeth.

Some of the cattle carried marks from every part of the range. Others were branded with the well-known T-7 that stood out huge on their hips. The calves hugging their sides were all branded Flying Spear. Peep jerked Torpedo to a halt. His whipping glance became a fixed stare of amazement.

Chapter Nineteen

No Names Mentioned

FOR AN INFINITY OF TIME Peep sat motionless as stone in the saddle, staring at the brands of the circling brutes. The discovery had stunned him. By the freshness of the work it was evident that those T-7's and Flying Spears had just been stamped onto the animals. A faint scent of burned hair hung over the herd. The brutes were still licking at the painful brands.

Dumbfounded though he was by the startling discovery, Peep, the cowman, could not but admire the skill of the rustlers. Apparently a wet blanket had been used to take the newness from their work. But who—? His mind was working like mad. Jumbled, twisted phrases, scraps of talk —gossip, conjecture, conclusion. Suddenly he recalled what Thompson had told him before the round-up about the six stolen calves being trailed across the Flying Spear. With that thought came another. A mental picture of the cabin in the canyon flashed into his mind.

He jerked straight in his stirrups, took careful note of his surroundings, his gaze whipping every coulee and wash, for sign of any movement. There was none, although he was positive that he was but a step behind the rustlers, if, indeed, sight of his approach had not interrupted them at their work. The smoke—

"So that's the game they're playing, is it?" he mused. "Right under our noses and making us like it. Well, I'll spike that in damned short order."

Cautiously alert to everything about him, ears tuned for the first alien sound, he rode on down the wash. Once he thought he caught the thud of galloping hoofs. But he could not be sure. Unarmed, and fully aware of his danger, he dared not investigate too closely.

As he expected, he presently came upon the remains of a chip fire which had been hastily banked with earth and which had given off the smoke that had attracted his attention. Dismounting, he walked about it, eyes searching for every sign. His glance fell upon a throw rope that no doubt the rustlers had overlooked in their haste to smother the fire and be gone at his approach. That glance became a stare. A slow pale shade blotted the tan from his cheeks. The throw rope was of hair, and through the center was braided a strand of yellow. There was but one such rope on the whole Satanka range—few, if any, like it on any range. The discovery staggered him. The presence of that rope beside an illegal chip fire on the open prairie was conclusive proof that the owner was guilty of rustling. And that rope belonged to Tommy O'Day! The hair rope their father had given him!

Peep's muscles jerked with violent emotion. Oblivious to any thought of danger, he fell to pacing about, torn between loyalty to the trust his father had imposed on him and a human longing to call his brother to account, erase this stain from the name of O'Day. One minute he resolved to bare the whole affair, charge Tommy openly with rustling and bring him to justice. The next moment he hated himself for even considering such a thing.

An hour passed thus. Still he could reach no decision. The light faded from the western horizon. Purple shadows deepened on the flats. Stars popped into the blue sky, turning slate. Out of the far dark came the yap of a coyote, ending in a long quavering wail. The zooming of a bullbat startled him to consciousness of things about him. He turned to where he had left Torpedo. The round corrals on Ragged Hound were sky-lined above him and stood out in silhouette against the lighter sky. It was in those corrals that his father had made his last ride. And in sight of them Tommy now—

"You are his keeper, Peep, like the Bible says," he seemed again to hear old Hank's voice drifting down from the corrals. "You are your brother's—"

In a half-dozen swift strides he was beside Torpedo, had caught up the reins and swung aboard. He roweled the brute into a stiff lope that pushed miles behind with amazing ease. He scarcely noticed the route they traveled in the darkness, leaving that to the sure-footed Torpedo, who picked his own course in and out of the greasewood up and down the steep banks of dry washes and across coulees. Not once did Peep draw rein until he swung down at the gate of the T-7.

Tying the blowing Torpedo at the hitch rail near the corral—along with several other horses—which caused him to wonder—he crossed the yard, stepped up onto the porch of the ranchhouse and knocked. Hope confronted him. But not the bedraggled Hope he had last seen at the Flying Spear. For she now wore a trim, starched house-dress which made her look even younger and lovelier. Made her eyes a deeper blue and accentuated the agate smoothness of her healthy color. The same shafts of gold streaked her mass of fluffy hair. He was conscious of her shrinking.

"Excuse me," he managed to blurt out, taken aback at this unexpected meeting with the girl. "I didn't—I wanted—"

"Peep O'Day!" she exclaimed. "Tommy—said—you—were—in—jail!"

"A lot of them think I am," he answered shortly, again sure of himself. "And they can keep on thinking so. But as far as you are concerned, I want you to know that there wasn't any charge against me—of any kind."

"No charge against you?" She thrilled him with a voice that trembled with eagerness. "Peep, are you telling me the truth?"

"Did I ever lie—to you?" Too late he caught the slip.

"Not—often," she countered. Almost happily, he

thought. "Oh, I'm so glad, Peep. Now you can come—"

"I want to talk to Jim," he changed the subject abrupt-ly, all too conscious of the loveliness of her, warned by a sense of insecurity that— "Can I see him?"

"Yes," regretfully, it seemed to him. "But if I were you —don't, now—I mean I wouldn't if I were you until I got Jim alone. He's terribly angry about that shooting scrape in Satanka. And Peep, you know how he is. He's almost unreasonable when he thinks he has a grievance. But if you've been exonerated—we can talk him out of it. Per-haps. Right now, all the ranchers who belong to the Cattle Association are in there."

"What are they doing here?" he demanded.

"They're going to put a range detective onto this rus-tling. Everyone is losing cattle, it seems. The whole coun-ty is up in arms. I'll call Jim if you insist—but if I were you—"

"I can see him tomorrow, I reckon. Who did he—did he get anybody in my place as foreman of the T-7?"

"Tommy, I guess," contritely. "He's—he's in there with them now."

"Has he—has Tommy been at the ranch all day?"

"No. He just came in. Why?"

"Nothing." Not by a flutter of an eyelash did Peep be-tray the emotion that surged through him with the sud-denness of a thunderbolt. Tommy, the foreman of the T-7! Tommy had just ridden in to meet the stockmen. Again, as always, it was Tommy. Tommy profiting through his own misfortune. Thought of the hair rope he had picked up beside the smothered chip fire, to which still clung the odor of smoke, sprang vividly to mind. And the conversation he had overheard at the cabin tucked away deep in the canyon. He opened his mouth to speak. A loud voice from within stayed his words.

"I'm not intimating anything. I'm saying right out— I'm plumb opposed to Tommy O'Day for this job of range detective."

"Then you're against me!" It was Thompson's voice now, raised in anger. "You aren't accusing Tommy—but, by God, you're insinuating. As the biggest taxpayer in this county I've got some rights. Tommy O'Day can't be held accountable for the trouble another jasper has had of late. I'm not mentioning any names, but—"

For all of him Peep's glance shot toward the girl. She had gone deathly pale; one hand clutched her breast. His eyes snapped back to the door from behind which the voices came.

"Do you mean Peep?" It was Tommy's voice now.

"I said I wasn't mentioning any names," Thompson boomed. "But the walloper I'm talking about went crazy with his Colt after being halter broke for years. It's in the —he's in jail now."

Peep jerked with violently straining muscles. The world seemed suddenly to have crumbled about his ears. Jim Thompson, whom he called friend, was deliberately branding him before everyone on the Satanka range as a rustler. By innuendo, to be sure. But nevertheless in such a way that no one could mistake whom he meant. Again his gaze sought that of the girl appealingly. Hers was soft, sympathetic. He looked away quickly. His eyes hardened, glittered like chilled steel. He struggled desperately against an anger that blazed up and threatened to consume him, against a wild and reckless notion to burst into the room, defy them all and make Jim Thompson eat his words. His face was bloodless, his lips braced.

"Don't—don't look that way," Hope pleaded in a tiny voice, catching hold of his arm. "It makes me—you can't blame Jim for thinking those things. Oh, Peep, if you didn't—"

"Didn't what?" He was scarcely conscious that he spoke, barely heard the words above the sluicing roar of hot blood that suddenly had set up an infernal pounding in his ears.

"Nothing," she returned sadly. "I guess—I guess I didn't understand it. You've—you lied to me, Peep. If you can explain, why don't you do it?"

"I will!" He pushed past her roughly into the house. In a half-dozen great strides he was across the room, had wrenched open the door.

Chapter Twenty

OUTCASTS

THE MOMENT WAS FRAUGHT WITH DANGER. Hope stood braced against the door, clutching her breast. Came a moment of deathly silence, broken only by the whir of Peep's spinning rowels. Then:

"Thompson," he shot out in a voice that was frozen, lifeless, "I'm the jasper you are insinuating has gone on the prod with his gun. And I just want to tell you—tell you in front of all these ranchers—tell everybody on the Satanka range that you're a liar, Thompson. A damned, dirty, sneaking liar! Do you get that straight, Thompson?"

Inside the room, Jim Thompson broke the tomblike silence that descended like a stroke. Fury welled up in him to contort his face. A violent oath left his lips.

"I thought you were in jail!" he jerked out in unison with Tommy.

"I'm not," Peep hurled back, stepping inside. "I'm here —here at the T-7 and plenty able to fight my own battles. As you know, Thompson."

"You can't call me a liar!" the furious cowman found voice to bawl. "I didn't mention your name. You'll swallow that or I'll—"

The movement Peep made was swift as that of a lunging puma. It carried him directly in front of the rancher to snap straight, spread-legged, rigid with bulging muscles. "You'll do what?" His voice was deathly quiet, yet it seemed to fill the great room, crash down on ears strained and waiting. "You'll do just what you've always done—" The sting of a blacksnake was in that tone—contempt, bitter, biting contempt, scorn. "You'll do nothing, you damned— Men who turn against their friends without giving them a hearing are cowards. Damned lousy cowards, Thompson!"

Deliberately turning his back on the cowman, who stood with great hands opening and closing convulsively, his weather-whipped face twitching with rage, choking sounds coming from his throat, he whirled on the others who had come up and edged back to stand motionless, transfixed as statues.

"You've been led to believe I'm the jasper who is rustling," Peep shot out. "It's a lie. I don't know any more about who is rustling than you do. But I do know what those missing critters are branded. Flying Spear and T-7! My brand and Jim Thompson's. Even in the face of this, I'm telling the lot of you—I never stole a critter. Never stole anything from anybody in my life. And I'm not going to be accused of it. And if there's a man on the Satanka who thinks he can say those things to my face, just one of you try opening your yawp!"

Clock-ticks passed, grave, ominous seconds without breath or motion, pregnant with the possibility of trouble. For there were men who were not cowards on the Satanka —men who had taken their toll of human life—men who many times had looked death in the face and smiled.

The stillness thickened, became tangible, clutched at men's throats and paralyzed their limbs. It was plain they wanted none of Peep O'Day, blazing mad. They had seen him in action, knew the thin-slitted lips, the glittering eyes; they read the danger signal in the iron muscles bulging in his rigid form.

The pantomime continued until it was breathless, the tinkle of a restless rowel, the slide of a nervous foot the only sound. Someone summoned the courage to move. The tension snapped. Tommy O'Day stepped to Peep's side.

"You don't know what you're saying," he remonstrated in a conciliatory manner. "You'd better keep your mouth shut until you're—"

Peep wheeled on him savagely. "That's why I'm in the fix I'm in—because I've kept my mouth shut. Shielding somebody else—but I'm through."

Tommy dodged, leaped back under the words that snapped and stung like a whiplash. "Through, do you hear? I can stand being called a crazy—a no-account—gunman. I can stand up under losing my job as foreman of the T-7 without a single chance to explain, but, by God, there isn't a man living who can call me a rustler and get away with it."

He took a step forward, his glittering eyes striving desperately to capture Tommy's gaze, which was whipping around like that of a trapped beast.

"I'm giving you fair warning, Tommy!" Peep's voice was purring soft yet seemed to rasp on overwrought nerves. "When you come looking for me as a rustler, don't come as a brother! You!" he hurled at the apopletic Thompson, "I'm telling you to your face—when we meet up again if you've shot off your trap like you have here tonight you want to come a-shooting! And," he strode to the door, spun about for a parting shot at the silent crew, "that goes for the whole damned lot of you!"

He kicked the door shut savagely behind him.

Just outside, Hope stepped aside for him to pass. Her face was flaming. Deep in her eyes glowed an inscrutable light. But then it couldn't be. He caught her gaze for a moment.

"I had to do it," he muttered contritely. "I had to tell them—to ease my—there wasn't any other way."

"You don't need to explain," she returned coldly. "I've been mistaken in you. I believe all that Jim said—and more!"

He stared at her in speechless amazement. Whirling, he stamped out of the house, crossed the yard to where Torpedo was tied to the rail, jerked loose the rein, mounted, and lifted the sorrel in a gravel-flinging lunge.

Outside the gate some impelling force shifted him sidewise in his saddle to look back. Hope stood framed in the
open doorway, gazing into the darkness, a slim figure
silhouetted against the light.

He snapped straight again in the saddle. A hand fell
down to twine nervous fingers in the mane of the sorrel.
The horse snorted and threw up its head defiantly. "Aren't
we in a hell of a mess now, old outlaw?" Peep whispered
bitterly to the ear that twitched forward and back. "My
own brother foreman of the T-7 in my place and a range
detective, watching me." Again the rowels sliced savagely
into Torpedo's sides. He lunged violently, straightened
out in a run. "Somebody is stealing cows and branding
them with my brand. Hope hates me. Old Jim, who I
thought was my best friend, is poisoning the ranchers
against me."

Again came the impulse to look back. Hope had not
moved, still stood framed in the lighted doorway. A queer
lump came up into his throat. A feeling of utter loneliness
assailed him. He had kept faith with his dead father only
to become an outcast. While Tommy—Tommy, for whom
he had sacrificed everything, had usurped his place and
raised no voice in his defense. The injustice of the thing
seared his soul. Thoughts of bitter vengeance ran riot
through his brain.

He swung about again, turned squared shoulders on
the figure of the silent girl.

"To hell with all of them," he growled, giving Torpedo
rein and streaking off into the night.

Chapter Twenty-One

DWINDLING HERDS

AUGUST BURNED ITSELF TO A CRISP on the Satanka. September sun lay like a scourge on the arid flats, blasting down from a cloudless sky that glittered like a sheet of tin, was coppery in its white heat. Hot breezes whining in the coulees rattled the parched grass and weeds, sucked the water from the creeks and reduced them to green-scummed, tepid pools, laden with insects. The flats danced and swayed as though a mirage in the relentless heat that drove man to shelter, sent the panting stock to the meager shade of cutbanks, where they huddled nose to tail, a united front against the tormenting swarms of flies and mosquitoes. Occasionally a wild-eyed steer, driven to desperation by the gnawing insects, would shake its head savagely, and dragging its horns through the brush, gallop bawling across the wastes. A stillness as oppressive as the heat itself hung like a pall over the alkali flats. The Satanka was a land bereft of beauty, sizzling, griddle-hot, radiating heat like the top of a stove.

Peep O'Day had dropped completely from sight. The night he had galloped away from the T-7, after calling Jim Thompson to account, was the last anyone had seen of him. It was rumored that he had left the range. No one knew positively. No one seemed to care particularly, unless perhaps it was Hope, who as the weeks passed grew strangely quiet and moody, or Bud Hamby, the sheriff, who divided his time between placarding the silent trails with reward notices and attempting to explain to an irate county attorney why he had allowed Peep to go scot-free.

Three days after the shooting affray the body of the man Peep was accused of killing had been found in a shed behind the Jumbo saloon in Satanka. In addition to the two forty-one slugs, which the doctor made oath he had taken from the man before his death, an autopsy revealed the startling disclosure that a third bullet had killed him instantly. And it too had been fired from a forty-one!

The clock-like routine of the big T-7 outfit that had prevailed under the foremanship of the close-lipped Peep had ceased altogether. Tommy O'Day was the recognized foreman of Jim Thompson's spread. But the exacting work—Tommy knew nothing of detail, cared less, and made no attempt at the thoroughness that had made Peep invaluable as a leader—together with that of under-cover detective for the Cattle Association, had reduced him to a nervous, haggard youth, constantly on his guard against something and openly suspicious of everyone. The ranchers, quick to notice the change that had come over him, remarked concerning it, and discussed it among themselves. Thompson answered their remarks with the explanation that Tommy's high-strung attitude was due to his indefatigable efforts to run down the rustlers, whose depredations not only were growing bolder each week, but whose wholesale operations threatened to force many of the stockmen to the wall, so great were their losses.

Tommy had leased an interest in the Flying Spear to Hi Binder, because, so he explained, due to Peep's mysterious absence and with so many other duties, he could not attend to things at his own ranch properly. At first—as a result of Peep's disclosure that part of the rustled cattle were branded Flying Spear—Binder was kept under close surveillance. But when Binder, of his own accord, came forward and organized a vigilance committee and demanded that every hoof in his pasture be checked, his name was immediately stricken from the list of suspects. A tally of his herd failed to reveal a single head that could even be so much as questioned.

Binder himself was thoroughly disliked by everyone on the range and especially by Jim Thompson and Hope, who—being fearful of implicating her foster father—never had mentioned to a soul the episode at the Flying Spear the night she had started from Satanka with Tommy. Although the other ranchers wondered at the bad feeling that existed between them, which no one made any attempt to conceal, none tried to find out its underlying cause. However, it did give rise to gossip, which quickly spread the length and breadth of the Satanka range. And like big Jim, not one of the other ranchers went out of his way to be civil to Binder. They were given small chance anyway, for he seldom left the Flying Spear and neither welcomed intimates nor sought new friendships.

Peep O'Day was the man everyone believed to be at the bottom of the high-handed thievery. His prolonged absence and the mystery surrounding his whereabouts only increased the suspicion against him. Friends who had clung for years to the grim-lipped young puncher began to entertain doubts. Enemies, and Peep's short abrupt manner had made many, were outspoken in their accusation. Gossip spread about him. Where direct charge was withheld, innuendo quickly showed the speaker to believe him guilty. And grim-faced posses, now riding the Satanka, never took to the trail without an unvoiced understanding that Peep was the man they sought.

The T-7 became the meeting point for harassed ranchers, who seemed to expect Thompson to bring the perpetrators of the rustling to justice. In this they were doomed to disappointment. They fell to grumbling, threatening to take matters into their own hands unless the Cattle Association, of which Thompson was the nominal head, and the law, as represented by Bud Hamby, quickly sifted the matter to the bottom.

Came mid-September. A cooling breeze had replaced the sickening wave that had hung incessantly in the coulees for weeks—a cooling breeze whipping in from the hills that carried a suggestion of early snow and sent anxious glances toward the horizon now banked with angry clouds. September was a month all stockmen feared on the Satanka. For early blizzards spelled death to undernourished stock. And many times a winter that started in September had lengthened mercilessly, not to be broken until the following May, or even June.

The shimmering heat waves that during the summer had veiled the flats had been replaced by smoke-blue air that brought the foothills deceptively near and reduced distance to a minimum. The horizon lengthened and became sharp-etched against a coppery sky.

Then one day, Ed Mann, of the Quarter-Circle L outfit, rode into the T-7 to find Thompson and Tommy engaged in an earnest conversation. Gaunt and grizzled was Ed, a man who had grown old on the Satanka. His weather-whipped face was corrugated with wrinkles, blackened by wind and sun. He carried his age well, but his hair-trigger temper had quickened with the passing years.

"Another ten head of my Quarter-Circle L stuff missing from my home pasture," he growled, swinging down to face the two, who stopped talking abruptly as he rode up. "The damned long-rope swingers are taking me for a cleaning, Thompson. The commission houses are going to raise hell. I've reached the end of my string. Now I'm saying to you, and everybody else on the Satanka, something has got to be done and done damned quick. I'm sick and tired of this fooling. Supposing we round up every man on the range and make them come clean. Somebody knows who is at the bottom of this rustling."

"That wouldn't get us anywhere," Thompson argued with a poor show of patience. "You can't force a man to tell anything he doesn't want to unless you've got a wedge to pry into him with. Why—we'd just get the horse laugh and make more enemies than we've got now. But where have you got any holler coming? You aren't losing any more critters than I am." He turned back to Tommy.

"Have you seen anything new?" he demanded.

Tommy's restive gaze whipped out across the smoke-blue flats. "I sighted a herd moving toward the river yesterday," he replied nervously. "I tried to catch up with it, but the riders had too much of a start. 'Course, at the distance I could tell only that they were cows. But my bet would be they were fresh she-stuff and calves the pace they were hitting."

"The hell you say!" Thompson exploded. "Why didn't you mention it before?"

"Because I aimed to get a line on it today." Tommy instantly became sullen. "We've had so many bum steers lately I didn't want to go half-cocked again. And—say," he blurted out hotly, "if you ain't satisfied with the way I'm doing, you know you can always—"

"You're doing all right," Jim put in hastily, before the glowering Mann could speak. "As good as any man could do under the circumstances. But I'll lope out myself after a while and take a look at things. Heading toward the river, huh?" He took Mann by the arm and started toward the ranchhouse. "By the way, Tommy," he threw back over his shoulder. "Hope has been riding a heap of late. Keep your eye on her a little closer. I'll tell her to stay nearer the ranch."

That had ended the talk. Tommy had watched the two until they had disappeared inside the house for a friendly drink, which Thompson always kept available. Then he had spun about angrily and disappeared into the barn. Some time later, Mann had come from old Jim's office, secured his horse, and despite Jim's booming attempts of assurance had ridden away muttering to himself.

An hour passed. Tommy tossed his saddle onto a horse and, without a word to anyone, swung out from the ranch at a high lope. Up in the office, big Jim Thompson had resumed the restless pacing that now had come to be constant with him.

Chapter Twenty-Two

"Why Did You Shoot Him?"

IT WAS THERE Hope found him presently. He started nervously and whirled as she entered. She cast him a strange inscrutable glance but said nothing.

"Tommy ran onto more fresh signs of rustling yesterday," he told her, obviously in explanation of his startled attitude. "The long-rope swingers are pushing stuff right under our noses. I'm warning you to watch where you're riding and don't get too far away from the ranch."

"Don't be silly, Jim," she laughed. "I'm not afraid of rustlers. I expect they'd rather steal cows than girls any time. But I'll be careful—just to keep you from worrying.. You're terribly nervous as it is. What's the matter with you lately?"

Ignoring her question as though he had not heard, he strode over to his desk and fell to tapping while he stared with unseeing eyes into space. She followed him to peck a kiss on his cheek and quietly left the room.

Later that day, apparently unmindful of the warning, she saddled her horse and headed away from the T-7 toward Ragged Hound.

"Jim is getting to be an old woman the way he watches out for me," she told her pony, which flicked its ears knowingly. "Imagine him thinking a rustler would bother me!"

At the round corrals she swung away from Surprise Creek and put her horse up a steep cow-trail writhing to the summit of the Ragged Hound buttes. After a stiff climb, the pony reached the top and stopped to blow. She shifted her weight to one stirrup to admire the view—a gorgeous panorama of color, blinding, ever-changing in the fierce light of late afternoon.

A horseman broke across her idle vision to bob up ahead on a parallel ridge. Even at the distance she recognized him, by the way he rode, as Jim Thompson. She cupped her hands and called, tried to attract his attention. But apparently he was out of earshot. She reined about and started down to meet him at the junction of the ridges and ride back to the ranch with him. She had gone but a short distance when a wisp of smoke, arising from a ravine below, caught her eye. She jerked rein to look. As she watched, a man straightened up. A calf leaped to its feet. She heard the faint report of a gun. A cow toppled over.

Her heart skipped a beat. She tried to scream a warning to her foster father. But he had ridden from sight over the brow of an adjoining butte. Throwing caution to the winds, she galloped recklessly down the trail in a wild attempt to cut in ahead and stop him.

Once out of sight of the man at the fire, she became frantic with fear. She reined about and drove her heaving pony back onto the ridge. Her one hope seemed to lie in reaching a high point where she could signal him. She reached the top as a second shot rang out. But now there were two horsemen in the ravine. As she watched, one wheeled and raced for the brakes. The other pitched forward in his saddle and slid to the ground beside the fire. A single cow and two freshly branded calves ran off a short distance to whirl and stare back at the strange proceedings.

"Jim! Jim!" she cried at the top of her voice, giving her pony rein and rowels to go thundering back down the trail.

No answer save the pounding hoofs and the echoes of her own voice beating back to her from the ragged buttes.

She negotiated the treacherous stretch between her and the fire at breakneck speed. Putting her horse into the ravine, she dragged it to its haunches and leaped to the ground. At her feet stretched Jim Thompson, blood trickling from a bullet wound in his temple!

Her mind seemed to have halted. She was scarcely aware of what she was doing. She looked about wildly. One greenish pool of water lay but a short distance away in the dusty bed of Surprise Creek. She ran toward it frantically, soaked her handkerchief, scooped up what water she could in her hat, and raced back. Vaguely she knew that sheer desperation was giving her strength for the task of restoring old Jim to consciousness. She fought grimly against a nausea that set things spinning about her. She rose up from bathing his forehead, to scream at the top of her voice. The cries and the flood of tears that fell unheeded across her cheeks seemed to relieve the tightness of her overwrought nerves.

Sight of a six-shooter at her feet cleared her brain. Although she knew little of firearms, she could not but notice the peculiar shape of the weapon; the smooth-worn cedar butt was round. Stooping, she picked it up and slipped it into her belt. Then she set about a desperate attempt to drag her foster father's limp form to his horse. Try as she would, her strength was not equal to the task. A stunning impotence assailed her. Her faculties seemed to halt with fatigue and fear. The nausea was returning. She sat flat down to ward it off.

The sound of a footstep brought her to her feet to stand swaying dizzily. How long she remained thus, fighting against a suffocating blackness that threatened to engulf her, Hope never knew. A cry sprang to her lips. Coming toward her, leading his mount, was a man. At first she thought it was Tommy. But this man's clothes were dusty, his chaps muddy and scarred with thorns. Tommy of late had been unusually careful of his appearance.

She could feel the hot blood rushing back into her icy cheeks. A mad torrent of emotions sent her eyes to the ground. A name formed on her lips.

"Peep O'Day!" she choked. "Where did you come from?"

"Hope!" burst from him. "Did you scream?"

"Yes!" Her senses were reeling, her efforts again suddenly incapable of fighting off the terrible nausea.

"What's wrong?"

"Jim's shot!" Her lips felt numb and cold. The man was swaying like a phantom before her eyes, the horizon beyond pitching, running in blurred and ragged lines.

"Old Jim shot!"

Dimly aware that Peep had dropped to his knees beside her foster father and was doing what he could, she let go of herself, crumpled to the ground. When again she was conscious of things, she heard his voice drifting to her from nowhere.

"How did it happen, Hope? Who did it?"

"You know—" Suddenly she was in full possession of her faculties.

"I know?" he repeated blankly. "What do you—how would I know?"

"Because you rode away from here a few minutes ago. I saw you." She ignored the aid he proffered and got to her feet. Where a moment before she was dizzy and helpless, she now felt strong and capable. "Don't say you haven't been here. And to think—in spite of everything—I had clung to a belief that you were not as bad as they all claimed!"

Her nerves were strung to the snapping point. For all her valiant efforts to control them she was swiftly working herself into a state of hysteria. "Why did you shoot him? Oh, why did you do anything like this? But you'll pay. I know—" Her eyes flew to his belt. He was without a holster or firearm of any sort. "I've got your—"

She was on the point of revealing that she had his gun— had picked it up beside the prostrate Thompson. But something checked her.

"You're nervous," he said coolly. "And mistaken. I didn't shoot Jim. I reckon he's only creased. But we had better get him where we can have Doc look at him."

She knew his suggestion was the one that she should follow, but an uncontrollable impulse to hurt him, to force him to confess the shooting, gripped her.

"How did you happen to be close enough to hear me scream if you know nothing about it?"

"We can thresh that out later. Right now old Jim needs attention. Give me a lift."

"You did it!" she accused stubbornly, making no move to help him.

"You don't believe that way down in your heart."

"I do!"

"But why should I shoot Jim?"

"For discharging you. For intimating that you were rustling. Didn't you threaten him that night you called him a—a liar? I can repeat your words. You said, 'When we meet up again, if you go to running off at the mouth like this, you want to come shooting.' They hurt me so I'll never forget them. And now—you've made your threat good. Never mind—I've got the gun that will convict the man who did it!"

"Let me see it," quickly.

"*No!*" His eagerness, she reasoned, was only further proof of his guilt. Seizing hold of her father's feet, she steadied them while Peep lifted him and carried him to his horse. Balancing the senseless cowman face downward across the saddle, he uncoiled his lariat and trussed him as best he could without cutting off his circulation.

"Do you think for a minute I would have the nerve to ride back and face you if I had shot Jim?" he asked when he had finished.

There was a pleading note in his voice, a wistfulness in his eyes which met hers so fearlessly, that made her for the moment regret her hasty words. She was on the point of admitting that in spite of the damning evidence she had not believed all she had said. Then her hand brushed the six-shooter in her belt. The wave of pity vanished. He had lied to her before! Securing the bridle reins of her father's pony, she mounted and, leading the brute, resolutely faced the trail toward the T-7.

"Where have you been so long?" she asked coldly after a time. "Did you know the sheriff was hunting you?"

"He's got to hunt somebody, hasn't he? I've been laying low trying to get some line on these rustlers."

"Is—is—that—all—you're—going—to—tell—me?" in a tiny voice, presently.

"What else do you want to know?"

"Nothing!" Dismounting, she bathed her father's head with her damp handkerchief and made him more comfortable in the saddle. The wound had stopped bleeding. Save for his awkward position he seemed to be resting easily.

When again they were on their way she did not return to the subject of his prolonged absence. He too rode in silence, apparently content to be silent and alone with his thoughts.

Chapter Twenty-Three

A Time for Brains

THEY JOGGED ON into the face of the setting sun that was bathing the flats with purple. As they topped the mesa above the T-7, and stood sky-lined for a moment, they were sighted from the ranch. Cowland has an inherent sense of danger. The punchers came out from the ranch at a gallop to meet them. Willing hands helped them along up to the ranchhouse, aided Peep in carrying old Jim into the house. Once help had arrived, Hope raced on ahead, and was waiting beside a ready bed. Few questions were asked, no explanations offered. If the punchers —many of whom had stuck by Peep despite the suspicion of him—even wondered, they gave no outward indication. It is cowland's way.

On the porch, as the group passed, sat two strangers. Peep recalled absently having seen them somewhere before. But in the excitement of the moment he could not place them. Nor did he have time to give them much thought.

"Call Tommy," Hope ordered, once her foster father had been stretched out on the bed and she had adjusted the pillows beneath his grizzled head.

"Tommy isn't here, Miss Hope," one of the punchers volunteered, awkwardly twirling his hat. "He rode away this morning, saying he was going up Ragged Hound way on a fresh rustler trail."

Hope's hand flew to her breast. Her glance flew to Peep. But the eyes that met hers gave no indication of what he was thinking. He might not have heard the cowboy for all the outward sign he gave.

Administering as best they could to the wounded Jim,

they presently had him showing signs of returning to consciousness. After a time he let forth a hollow groan. His
eyelids fluttered open slowly. Wild eyes whipped about
the room. Then, as the dullness of insensibility vanished,
they came to rest on Peep. Anger flared up to blaze in
their depths. Big Jim struggled violently to rise. Strong
hands held him down. He tried to speak. Presently his
choking gutturals became coherent, although they were
barely audible.

"Don't—let—that—jasper—go!" he gasped out. "He—shot
—me!" The effort was too great. The wide eyes became
glazed, fluttered shut. Big Jim straightened out with a
groan, again unconscious.

Swift, furtive glances passed between the men. Peep's
face only whitened, his lips set in grimmer lines. Clock-
ticks passed; silence almost tangible descended on the
group. Hope was the first to recover her wits.

"One of you boys get started to Satanka for the doctor
and the sheriff," she cried hysterically. "Another one of
you ride over to the Circle L and ask Mrs. Mann to come
over and help us. The rest of you—" Her eyes lashed the
awkwardly waiting group, which made no effort to move,
nor carry out her commands. "Get out!" she blazed.

They fell back before her outburst, trooped from the
house. All but Peep. He stood motionless as stone, his eyes
glittering strangely.

She straightened up, squared her shoulders defiantly.
"Go!" she choked.

"After Jim asking that I be held—for shooting him?"
His voice was ominously quiet. She knew the danger signal of Peep O'Day boiling with reckless anger. "And you
thinking me guilty."

"I'm giving you—giving you a chance to escape."

Even as she gave utterance to the words she was ashamed
of them. Peep O'Day escaping from anybody!

"Thanks just the same," he was saying in a tone that

maddened with its calm and quiet, "but I haven't done anything to run for. I did see Jim up there on Ragged Hound—and he saw me. But that isn't any proof that I shot him by a jugful. You know way down in your heart you don't believe I did—or you wouldn't be telling me to go. You hate a quitter just as bad as I—"

"How can I help but believe it?" She struggled desperately to hold back the tears that were stinging on her lashes. "Everything is against you: your unexplained absence, your gunplay, those forty-one bullets. Yet in spite of it, I'm offering you a chance to—"

"Show yaller," he finished scornfully. "And I'm not going to."

He got no further. A jangle of rowels, the thud of running feet cut him short. The door was flung open violently. Tommy, white-faced and excited, burst into the room.

"Jim's shot!" he panted. "Who did it? How—"

Unconsciously Hope's startled gaze flew to Peep. Tommy's eyes followed.

"You?" he gasped.

"It looks like it," Hope admitted haltingly. "This gun I found beside Jim will prove it." She pulled the six-shooter from her belt and passed it over to Tommy. The hand he reached for it trembled. Sight of it drained the last vestige of color from his cheeks.

Peep too felt the icy wave that blotted the tan from his own face. The gun was a forty-one. No need to look at the initials on the rounded stock. They could be nothing but J.T. It was the Colt his father had given him. The gun he had lost in the Jumbo at Satanka—had attempted to recover from Binder's holster only to find that he had snatched its mate with an H.O. in the bull's-eye on the stock.

"Do you—" Hope's voice was tremulous, little more than a frightened whisper. "Do you recognize it?"

Tommy's head jerked nervously in acquiescence. "It's—

it's Paw's."

"Is—it—Peep's?" Hope choked.

"Yes."

"Then you are guilty!" There was anguish, heartbreak in her hysterical cry. "Arrest him, Tommy. I've already sent for the sheriff."

Tommy made no move. Nor did his gaze meet the steady one Peep had focused upon him. "It's pretty hard to—to arrest your own brother," Tommy muttered.

"Especially when a jasper happens to know that his own brother isn't guilty." Peep's voice seemed brittle, cracked like ice.

"How can you—how dare you deny it any longer?" Hope cried, her eyes, now filled with tears, searching his face.

"Well, I can. Simply because I did not shoot Jim Thompson!"

Tommy jerked himself straight. "As range detective for the Cattle Association I reckon it's my duty to arrest you, Peep," he blurted out.

"Well, why don't you do it?" Peep challenged coolly.

Tommy's answer was to go for his gun. It flashed to the rim of his holster. A scream escaped Hope's whitened lips. She lunged forward, seized Tommy's arm.

But Peep made no move. He stood as though transfixed. Now he had captured Tommy's roving gaze, held it mercilessly, his glittering steel eyes flecked with pinpoints of flame.

"You wouldn't stop me with that forty-five if I wanted to go," he taunted purringly. "And it's damned lucky for you that it is me you're messing up a draw on instead of a real killer with blood in his eye. He'd take that gun away from you and— Use your head, if you've got any. It's time for brains instead of gunplay on the Satanka. There's always got to be a motive for any crime. Tell me—just what would be my reason for shooting Jim Thompson?"

"Why—why—everybody knows there is bad blood between you," Tommy flashed, taking courage from the feel of the steel in his hand. "Everybody heard you warn Jim— to come a-shooting when you met up. You're suspected of rustling. Mebbeso Jim caught you branding a critter and—"

"That's exactly what did happen," Hope put in excitedly. "He was—"

"If you both are dead certain it was me, that's all there is to it, I reckon," Peep remarked bitterly. "And Tommy allows it is his duty to arrest the jasper who did it. So—"

"What the hell are you driving at?" Tommy demanded in a high-pitched, unnatural tone.

"You know, you—" Peep spun on his heel. Without so much as a glance at the forty-five covering him, he strode over to the door. "You're a damned bluff, Tommy. Always have been and always will be. You've had your chance. Take it or leave it. But I'm telling you this—once and for all—if you're so dead anxious to do your duty as a range pussy-foot, why don't you arrest the walloper who really did shoot Jim Thompson?"

Tommy's gun wavered, then slowly slid back into its holster. His ashen face started to twitch convulsively. Hope stared, wide-eyed, uncomprehending. She tried to speak. Words failed her. Withering Tommy with a scornful glance, she sprang over to the door just as Peep wrenched it open, strode through, and slammed it violently in her face. She backed against it, panting, furious with anger.

"You—you—coward!" she blazed through set teeth at Tommy. The taunt stung him to action. He seized hold of her arm, attempted to push her aside roughly.

"Don't you dare touch me," she cried. "I'll—you—" She choked with fury.

Tommy edged off to stare at her in blank amazement. "A minute ago you told me to arrest him," he blurted out savagely. "And now you're keeping me from it. He shot

Jim. He's a rustler. It's hard, but—"

"I'm not so dead sure about it now," she said slowly, gathering her temper-strewn thoughts, but making no move to stand aside for him to pass. "And I'm giving you fair warning. Don't you dare arrest him until after I've had a talk with Jim. I'm going to get to the bottom of this thing once and for all. And let me tell you here, I don't believe—" She stopped abruptly and crossed the room with eyes suddenly dimmed with a blinding flood of tears. She stared out upon the purple world of sage and grease-wood, growing tall, ominous in the evening shadows that seemed to lengthen momentarily.

Chapter Twenty-Four

The Missing Link

Once he was outside the room, Peep O'Day stood listening for a moment. The words of the two within drifted plainly to him. But with a natural aversion to eavesdropping of any kind, even when it affected him so vitally, he passed on quietly, and quit the house.

Just outside on the porch, he again came upon the two strangers, who had not moved. In the failing light he recognized them. They were the two commission men he had overheard talking to the cashier in the bank at Satanka the night of his release from jail.

Peep started off the porch, then spun about and planted himself before them.

"You won't be able to see Jim, if that is what you are waiting for," he told them curtly.

"Is he hurt badly?" one inquired, visibly anxious.

"Just creased, I reckon. But—what do you want? Is there anything I can do—"

"It's personal," shortly.

"It's about that five-thousand-dollar mortgage you were talking over with the cashier of the bank at Satanka, isn't it?"

"Yes, but—"

Peep thought quickly. To allow a foreclosure on the T-7 and a tally of the herds now would upset the desperate expediency upon which he suddenly had resolved. He seized upon the first idea that popped into his mind to avert the impending catastrophe. The cashier at Satanka had told him his check was good for any amount up to six thousand dollars. That the check would be—

"Come on down to the bunkhouse!" He whirled and

stepped off the porch. The two arose at the abrupt summons. Questioning glances passed between them but they made no move.

"I'll pay that note and take over that mortgage," Peep threw over his shoulder as he strode away. "And you won't have to worry Jim."

The two followed with alacrity, their faces now wreathed with smiles. Inside the bunkhouse, Peep was as good as his word. He wrote the first check in the new book the cashier had given him, scrawled in pencil the sum that took almost the entire stake his father had left him. But if he gave the thing a thought he did not show it. Under the loud thanks of the two, he was mute, moodily silent, scarcely hearing.

Half an hour later the three mounted and left the T-7 together. At the gate the two commission men shook hands with Peep, again voiced their thanks, and turned their mounts in the direction of Satanka. Peep watched them until they were but dots in the twilight, then whirled his own horse and set out up Surprise Creek toward the Flying Spear.

"Just once more," he muttered aloud to set his horse's ears flicking, "and then I'm through with lying for a while." He stroked the neck of the brute, which arched proudly under the caress. "I don't suppose that brother of mine would care about trading, but—" He leaned over to size up the animal he rode. It was Tommy's horse. And he had ridden it purposely away from the T-7 although it lacked the gait, the fire, and the speed of his own top mount, Torpedo. "You know, horse, there's an old saying: 'You've got to catch a fox by playing a fox's game.' I wonder if we're going—"

The pony pushed the miles beneath its hammering hoofs. The huddled buildings of the Flying Spear came in sight, vague, unreal in the swiftly falling darkness. Peep drew rein on the pony, which fought the bit savagely with the slackened pace. But apparently the thoughtful Peep was in no hurry, for the nearer he advanced to the now dimly outlined buildings, the slower they moved.

After a time they were through the gate, had moved slowly past the barn. Then they were before the squatty rough-board ranchhouse. Peep swung down.

"Howdy, Binder," he greeted.

Binder slouched to his feet from the doorstep where he was sprawled, smoking.

"Howdy," he grunted unpleasantly.

"Where's all the men?" Peep inquired, bracing himself against his mount's shoulder, and twisting a cigaret, the reins in his hand.

"Just—riding. Ain't come in yet." He peered through the mellow twilight at the foam-splattered pony. Then his gaze flashed back to Peep. "You're Peep," he snarled.

"My God, are we going through all that again?" Peep groaned with mock despair. "You ought to be able to recognize my horse even if you never can recognize me." Yet he was thankful for the wan light which made too close an observation impossible.

"You might be Tommy," Binder conceded grudgingly. "My eyes ain't just what they used to be. But you two look so much alike I'll bet your old man had a hard time knowing you apart. Come on in." He slouched through the open doorway. Ground-picketing his horse, Peep followed, striving thoughtfully to simulate Tommy's careless gait, the little mannerisms he knew so well.

Inside, Binder kicked a chair across to him. Peep dropped into it, sprawling, as the lazy Tommy would have done.

"Your horse is the only way I can tell you apart," Binder was saying. "Have you heard any word from that brother of yours?"

"No. And I don't want to." Tommy himself would have started at the likeness to his own sullen voice issuing from

Peep's lips.

Several minutes passed in silence, Peep dragging on his quirley, Binder eyeing him furtively through the murk of the cabin's interior. Presently Binder shifted restlessly. "Well, what do you want? Spit it out?"

Determined to plunge in recklessly, win or lose, Peep pushed his chair back farther into the shadows and tilted carelessly against the wall.

"Of course you haven't forgotten that I lost that thousand to you at poker?"

"Huh!" Binder's grunt warned Peep. "Of course I haven't forgotten it. But wasn't it—we settled that up with this lease and that cabin."

"Yeah, I know, because I didn't have the money handy right then." Now Peep was a little surer of his ground. "I'm going to pay you off. I aimed to do it anyhow, and now—"

"I always said you were the right kind, kid." Of a sudden Binder's voice was cordial, gloating. Peep could almost sense him rubbing his fat, greedy hands. And he breathed easier with the knowledge that at last the fellow's obvious suspicion was allayed. "But there is a condition, Binder. If I fork over that thousand, you're going to release me from all the dealings with you."

"We ain't good enough for you, huh?" Binder snorted explosively. "Just who in the hell do you think you are anyway? You're into it now as deep as I am. How the hell do you think you're going to quit?"

"That's for you to figure out." Confident that his ruse was working, Peep hung onto his soaring spirits with an effort. "If it is worth that thousand, all right. If not, we'll just—"

"Don't get in a sweat. Keep your shirt on. There might be some way. Just what is it you want to get out of?"

The point-blank question almost upset Peep's calculations. Attempting the deception as he had on sheer nerve, trusting only to luck to pull him through, he was unprepared to be quizzed too closely. And now—he sifted his mind for an answer to Binder's question—an answer that would suffice, yet throw the fellow off.

"You know as well as I do," he countered lazily after a time.

For all his outward calm, Peep held his breath waiting for an answer. But if Binder even noticed, he gave no sign. Peep was conscious of a feeling of great relief. For Binder himself was saving the day.

"That cabin deal, for instance?" Binder was saying. "How in hell was I to know when you stashed us up there that it belonged to Jim Thompson? But it makes a fine place to work that stuff at night!"

"That's one thing," Peep encouraged as the fellow fell silent. "There's others. You name them so there won't be any misunderstanding. I'll tell you if you miss anything."

"I suppose you mean that T-7 stuff you've turned over? It's all branded Flying Spear. You know where it is. You can't get out of that no matter what—"

"But I want to square up everything and shoot clean from now on." Peep imitated Tommy's nervous fidgeting.

"And squeal," Binder snarled. "Not by a damned sight you don't. You're into it just as deep as we are, I tell you, and by God you'll—"

"Don't forget that killing." Satisfied that he was on the right track, Peep fell back upon the conversation he had overheard between Tommy and the fellow that night at the cabin in the canyon.

"You're done for if you ever open your yawp about that," Binder warned. "Damn you, this country won't be big enough for us if—"

"I didn't say I'd mention it," Peep denied hastily. "But they haven't got my—haven't got Peep behind bars yet and he isn't as crazy as you and your punchers would like to make yourselves believe he is. Just supposing he proves

that he didn't kill that jasper? Then where are we setting?"

"Well, he can't prove that I did," Binder guffawed
evilly. "I was just a little too damned smart for them. I shot
him with a forty-one too."

"That was pretty smart," Peep agreed, striving to keep
a sudden exultant quaver from his husky voice. "But I
didn't know you had a forty-one."

"I haven't." Binder closed up like a clam. Peep deftly
dropped the subject, conscious that he had gone as far as
he dared along the trail.

A moment of silence passed. Peep strove desperately to
keep his own riotous thoughts from making conversation
strained.

"Jim Thompson was shot over on Ragged Hound today," he ventured after a time.

"That isn't any of my affair," Binder flashed. "Nor
yours either for that matter. You didn't shoot him, did
you?"

"No," slowly. "Did you?"

"It's none of your damned business," Binder exploded.
"Your measly thousand don't cut you in deep enough to
jerk me up on the carpet and try to put me through a
third degree. I'm keeping my own counsel. And if you're
smart, you'll do the same. You've got no bellyache coming.
You're getting your split for turning stuff branded T-7 over to me to trail into those brakes and re-run into a Flying
Spear. If you've lost your guts, I'll just take your thousand and we'll call it quits. But as long as you stick around
this range, there'll be a walloper just behind you with a
bead and itching to drop you the minute you open your
chops."

In a flash the whole thing was revealed to Peep. As he
had hoped, deliberately risked trouble for, the fellow had
unwittingly supplied the link that had defied his best efforts. Now that it was in his possession, he cast about for

some way to bring a showdown. But he cursed himself now for his idiocy, for his utter disregard of danger that amounted to frank foolhardiness. As usual he was unarmed.

Ever a man of sudden decision, which many times caused him regret, but which again amounted to a snap judgment that was remarkable, he determined to play a reckless impulse that flashed into his mind.

"Light a lamp," he suggested. "And I'll give you that check for a thousand."

"Check?" Suspicion was strong in Binder's query. "Do you think I'm just plain damned fool. I don't want any check."

"It's all I've got. Besides, knowing we're dealing together here on the Flying Spear, the bank won't think anything of it." Peep paused, waiting for Binder to speak. But the fellow remained silent. "Light a lamp anyhow. We'll auger the thing. This damned dark gives me the creeps."

It was what Tommy would have said. And it was obvious that if Binder still retained any suspicion as to his real identity, that proposal swept it aside.

"Got you leary and ready to break, have they?" The piggish-faced man arose and moved off to comply with the request. Peep too arose and walked over to the stove. Binder stooped to scratch a match against it. Peep's fist shot out like a piston. Flesh cracked on flesh. A sickening sound. Binder lurched backward, under a terrific impact, threw out his arms and went sprawling to the floor. Peep leaped above him, started to stoop.

The clatter of hoofbeats descended upon him. Binder's men, galloping toward the cabin, flashed through his mind. He jerked straight above the fallen Binder. His brain worked with lightning rapidity. For them to find their chief unconscious would ruin his whole scheme. The hoofbeats were pounding nearer. He waited, breathlessly, listening. The thunder stopped. Saddle leather creaked as the punchers swung down. A grim smile quirked the corners of Peep's lips. He strode to the door.

"It's Tommy, jaspers," he shouted. "Been waiting here for you to show up. Binder left word for you all to shag it up to the cabin in the canyon as quick as you came in. I turned over some new T-7 stuff that has to be worked pronto. Binder wants to slap an iron on 'em yet tonight. Get going! And sift plenty of dust."

The ruse worked far better than Peep had dared hope. Muttering curses among themselves, the punchers swung wearily back into their saddles, jerked about their head-fighting horses and roweled away. Peep stood listening until the hoofbeats had become a throb on the distant night air. Then he turned back into the cabin and lighted the lamp, which he placed in the center of the table. This done, he crossed over to Binder, who had not moved, and relieved him of his gun. He looked at the Colt carefully. But it was a forty-five caliber. Shoving it into his empty holster, he strode over, picked up the bucket of drinking-water and sloshed it into the unconscious Binder's face, leaving him drenched and dripping. Chuckling inwardly at the sorry spectacle the fellow presented, he went back to his chair, dropped wearily into it, twisted another cigaret, and settled down to wait Binder's return to consciousness.

Minutes dragged by, minutes filled with ominous portent to nerves jangling with apprehension. The thin chirp of a cricket beneath the woodbox sounded shrilly in the piercing silence that pervaded the place. The gnawing of a mouse grated jarringly. The light, fanned by a cool breeze, flickered fitfully, set shadows to dancing grotesquely on the wall. Outside a bull-bat darting for insects zoomed like a plane. Somewhere far out on the night-wrapped wastes a dog was barking in answer to a challenge from a distant canine. A coyote was wailing, its eerie howl rising and falling on the night air. Far down on the flats a steer was bawling. An answer drifted back in the rumbling challenge of a bull.

For all he could do, Peep's nervousness increased as he waited. He struggled to control himself. He strained with bated breath to catch the first untoward sound from out of the night. Yet his heart seemed to pound the louder in his ears, as he strove to listen. The peaceful sounds from without somehow keyed his overwrought nerves, filled him with a haunting sense of impending trouble. Presently he shook himself, got to his feet, and strode over to stand above the prostrate Binder.

In the wan light he caught the glint of the fellow's open eyes.

"What—what hit me?" Binder choked.

"I did," Peep returned coolly, jerking the forty-five to the rim of his holster as the fellow lurched up to his feet, to stand clutching his head and reeling dizzily. "I was just toning you down to get ready for a trip. A trip you and I are taking together."

"You ain't Tommy," Binder exploded in the light of sudden discovery. "You're that—Peep O'Day!"

"At last you are showing signs of real intelligence," Peep mocked. "And I'll say this much—it takes a haystack falling down on you to make you see things. But as long as you've finally figured out that I am really Peep, and not Tommy, I'm much obliged to you for giving your hand away so dead easy."

"You'll pay dear for this," Binder roared. "And let me tell you—if anything happens to me, that damned double-crossing Tommy is into it a sight deeper than I am. I'm not—"

"We'll see about that, too," Peep cut him short. "Rattle your hocks for the barn, jasper. We're going places—fast."

Chapter Twenty-Five

SHOWDOWN

WORD OF THE ATTEMPT on the life of Jim Thompson spread like wildfire over the Satanka range. It was the spark for which the seething region had been waiting—to set it off—to turn it into a tinderbox of hatred and bloodshed. Grim-faced men threw down their tools, left their work, saddled their fastest mounts, looked to their cartridge belts, filled up their gun chambers, and set out post-haste for the T-7. They rode savagely, mercilessly—the way men of the range ride when they are angry.

By the time Peep had ridden into the ranch with Binder, lanterns twinkled back and forth across the yard. A stern-faced, silent crowd was milling restlessly about or squatting on their heels talking in guarded tones. Saddled horses squealed and kicked at the jammed hitch rails. Short as had been the time since his departure, the doctor, who had rushed to the ranch from Satanka, had put in an appearance. After a careful examination he had pronounced Jim Thompson only slightly wounded and out of danger, barring, of course, unforeseen complications.

Bud Hamby, the sheriff, was there too. He swaggered about in the deadly earnest crowd, laughing boisterously at his own attempts at humor, quizzing the thoroughly aroused ranchers and deftly pumping the excited Tommy, whose volubility was evidence of his nervousness.

The sound of new hoofbeats out of the night announced Peep's approach with Binder. At the point of a gun he forced the fellow to dismount at the corrals and prodded him toward the house, ablaze with light. At the steps leading onto the porch, Bud Hamby held high a lantern to throw the full light in Peep's face.

"You!" the sheriff blurted out. "So the chase is ended! Throw down your gun, you. You're under arrest."

The others came on a run to close in at Hamby's outburst. Peep saw the lanterns bobbing in from every direction. He gave no thought to resistance. A wan smile moved from his thin lips. Without a word, he passed over, butt first, the forty-five he had taken from Binder.

"So I'm under arrest again, am I?" he asked blankly. "What for this time—Mister Hamby?"

"For that Jumbo killing," the sheriff bawled furiously. "And for the shooting of Jim Thompson. You're going to Satanka—back to jail. Damn you, you've led me a merry chase—but—"

"But I had to ride into the T-7 before you could find me. Are you still dumb enough to charge that Jumbo killing against me?" Peep snorted disgustedly.

"You're damned right I am. And what's more, the law will hang you for it—mark my words—I've been hunting you for weeks."

"You must of been hunting hard," Peep said. "I'm right sorry to cause you all this trouble. Now if you'd let me know I'd of— And your chances of hanging me are mighty slim, Bud, much as you'd like to. Hold your horses for a minute. Then, after you hear what I've got to say, if you still want to arrest me, all right—but—Doc got here all right?"

"Yes." The doctor himself, attracted by the loud voices, answered from the doorway.

"Is there any chance of me seeing Jim for a few minutes?" Peep asked.

"Why, yes. That is, if you'll promise not to excite him any. He's—"

"You and Tommy come along with Doc and me," Peep ordered the gaping Hamby. "And you're going too, jasper." He poked the sullen Binder in the ribs with his fist.

They filed into the house, the doctor leading the way. Hamby, his gun clutched in his hand, was a step behind Peep and Binder, while Tommy moved along silently in the rear.

Thompson stared up through glazed eyes as they trooped into the room, noisy in their tip-toed attempts at quiet in their high-heeled boots and rowels. His eyes darted along the row of faces, shadowed in the wan light of a lamp turned low on the dresser. Anger flared into their depths as they finally came to rest on Binder. Then they roved on to Peep. Big Jim jerked bolt upright in bed. "You—you—" came chokingly from his lips.

"Just take her easy now, Jim," Peep soothed. "This here is going to turn out all right. I'm in the know. Thought I'd ride back and tell you, and Hamby here, who shot you."

"You shot me," Thompson thundered, while the doctor tugged at his arm trying to force him down in the bed.

"Yeah?" The friendliness left Peep's voice, which suddenly became icy, merciless in its coldness. He whirled on Tommy, who stood by nervously, his gaze darting furtively about the room. "Have you got the gun Jim was shot with?" Peep asked quietly. "The one Hope found at—" His manner was casual, maddeningly confident. Of all the group he seemed the least perturbed.

With fingers that seemed to tremble Tommy produced the forty-one that Hope had given him but a short time before in that very room. Hamby reached for it, moved over to the dresser, turned up the light, and examined it closely.

"See anything familiar about it?" Peep asked coolly.

"Sure I do," Hamby shot back. "It's yours."

"You seem to get dumber every day, Bud," Peep exploded. "You say this forty-one is mine. If that's the case, you did the shooting. Because you've had my forty-one in the desk in your office ever since the night you had me in jail."

Hamby winced, started to speak, caught himself, and stared hard at Peep for an instant. "You don't need to—" he began furiously. "But—by God, you're right—I have got your forty-one in Satanka. But whose gun is this?"

"Mine!" Thompson himself answered the question in a voice that quavered with rage.

"Yours?" Although Peep had half expected it, he found himself startled at the discovery. "What are the initials on your forty-one, Jim?"

"There aren't any initials on it."

Peep was prey to a quick and satisfying feeling of relief. If Thompson had never seen the initials he certainly could not know that the guns had been exchanged and that this one, now in Hamby's hands, was not his forty-one.

"Do you happen to know the history of that gun, Jim?" Peep inquired, enjoying the nervousness of the group as he deliberately drew out the questioning.

"I didn't know it had any history," Thompson snarled. "But we're only wasting time. Arrest him, Hamby—" He locked gazes with Peep. His fell before the eyes that met his steadily, unafraid.

"That gun was found among Paw's things when he died," he muttered. "I was a kid—I just simply took it."

Peep could have shouted for joy with the surge that rushed through him. Hank O'Day had killed Thompson's father—had worked for years alongside of the son, who, apparently had no knowledge of the affair.

"Where has your forty-one been, Jim?" he asked quietly, after a time.

"I don't know," sullenly.

"Come clean," Peep shot out significantly.

"I don't know, I tell you."

Peep faced Hamby, who was watching him like a hawk.

"He's covering up, Bud," he accused. "He won't talk, so I'm going to. Binder here took Jim Thompson's forty-one away from him in a fight in a canyon east of the Flying Spear the night of that Jumbo scrap."

"You're a liar," Thompson shouted. "Damn you, you can't—"

"You're damned right you are," Binder suddenly jerked from his sullenness to bawl. "I'll—I'll—"

"You'll swing for murdering your helpless pal, that's what you'll do," Peep silenced him coolly. "You bragged about it—to me. Bragged about how smart you were to use a forty-one. Odd caliber gun, huh? Only two on this range. Bud, the first two forty-one slugs in that jasper you accuse me of killing were put there by me and Jim Thompson, one each. That's why Jim won't talk. He thinks he killed the walloper. But he didn't—not by a damned sight, he didn't—Hi Binder killed him. Killed him in cold blood—finished him off with a third slug from Jim's own forty-one." He reached out and pulled Binder back as the fellow started to spring forward. "And what's more—Hi Binder shot Jim Thompson!" Binder whirled, cursing. Peep squared off and would have floored him with a blow had not Hamby intervened. He sprang between the two of them, his gun muzzle jerking nervously.

"Spill your guts if you really got something to say," he rasped out at Peep.

Peep's only answer was to twist a cigaret with deliberate and moddening calm. The tick of a clock on the dresser boomed on overwrought nerves. The rattle of rowels on nervously shifting feet crashed down upon the tense group. Still Peep dallied, obviously hugely enjoying the pantomime.

Presently the cigaret was rolled. He pinched the end, struck a match, held it in his cupped hands until it was almost burned out. Then he applied it to the quirley, took a long deep drag, exhaled it through his nostrils.

The tension tightened until nerves neared the breaking point. A falling pin would have reverberated like a ton of bricks.

Hamby stirred, broke the horrible stillness. "For God's sake, talk, you—you—"

"Killer?" Peep reminded him grimly. "Why don't you finish it? That's what I am. To your way of thinking. But what's the matter with you fellows' nerves? I'm the one who's been hunted. I'm the rustler on the Satanka. Yet I'm not all riled up and skittish. I'm not scared. You're a packed of damned cowards, all of you. Yaller—but—"

He grinned broadly into the white-hot face of Hamby, started to speak again only to fall silent. He was on the point of revealing that Thompson had been wounded with the forty-one he himself had dropped on the floor during the fracas at the Jumbo. But he thought better of it. Nor did he mention a fact that suddenly had come to him with startling clearness! Binder had had both his forty-one and Jim Thompson's in his belt at the Flying Spear the night he had snatched the H.O. gun!

Then suddenly Tommy found his voice, tremulous, high-pitched, a mere semblance of his natural voice. "How come you to be hanging around up where Jim was shot?" he demanded.

"Up where Jim was shot? What do you mean?" Peep jerked with muscular violence. "You yaller coyote," he snorted. "To think— Damn you, are you turning against your own kin just to— I'll tell you how come. I was up there watching Binder kill a cow and brand her calf!"

"I only wanted to see justice done," Tommy muttered. "I—the Cattle Association—"

Chapter Twenty-Six

A Sheep on a Cow Range

FOR A MOMENT utter silence fell on the group, the vast and awful silence found in chambers of the dead. The six stood as though transfixed. The flickering coal-oil lamp kept shadows playing over their grim, set faces. From without drifted voices, guarded voices that relieved the tension in that nerve-taut room.

Peep was the first to move. The eyes he turned on Tommy glittered coldly.

"Justice, hell," he spat at his brother. "Nobody wants to see justice done—least of all you. But you're going to get it, whether you like it or not. Because I'm the black sheep on this cow range. I'm out to clear the name of Peep O'Day—and you'll all be trying to dodge this justice you're craving so hard before I get through."

He took a threatening step. Tommy recoiled, his face bloodless, his tongue wetting dry lips nervously.

"You heard what I said, Hamby," Peep snapped out. "I'm laying charges—file 'em. Damn you, you couldn't find things out for yourself, so I'm telling you. I saw Binder rustling today—and so did old Jim. That's what the shooting was over. Jim didn't dare squeal who did it because he was afraid they'd yank him up for murdering that fellow I shot down in the Jumbo. Hi Binder is the long-rope swinger on the Satanka!"

"The hell you say?" Hamby gulped dubiously. "You can't— Damn you, Peep O'Day, you're the— Why, Binder is head of the Vigilantes. He's been helping me, working with me. You can't pull that—"

"Yes, and this same Hi Binder has been stealing the range ragged under your dumb nose," Peep cut him short sourly. "He's been re-running T-7's into Flying Spears."

"There wasn't a stolen critter in his stuff when we tallied 'em," Hamby shouted belligerently. "How do you figure that, jasper? Where's his rake-off, if he is rustling? Punchers don't rustle for their health. Besides, Flying Spear is your brand. Binder is working for you, that's what he's doing."

"Like hell he is," Peep flared. "Any time I hire a— He killed that jasper I shot in the Jumbo so he could frame me for murder. He forced Tommy to give him that lease to the Flying Spear because the kid owed him money— a thousand bucks he'd lost at poker—that's what the rumpus was about that night in Satanka. I horned in. But I guess it wasn't my turn to beller. Of course you couldn't find any rustled stuff in Flying Spear pastures. But you found a lot of T-7 strays, didn't you?"

"Yes," Hamby admitted grudgingly. "But just because there are strays in a fellow's pasture don't mean—"

"You're so dumb it hurts, Hamby," Peep snorted. "A T-7 runs into a Flying Spear without a blemish or a misplaced hair. Knowing this, Binder had Thompson plumb on his hip. The stuff he couldn't get away with quick, he slapped a T-7 onto. Nobody thought anything of that. There are T-7's strung from hell to breakfast in this county. But he branded the slicks Flying Spear. If he couldn't run the brands on the she-stuff, he shot them. He trailed the rustled critters to the brakes—where he has a cabin hide-out—Thompson's line camp—"

"And for all your wild ideas I'm still claiming that Hi Binder, or nobody else, no matter how smart they are, could have done anything with stolen critters packing your brand and Jim Thompson's," Hamby shot back furiously.

"He could pick up any stuff on the Satanka that would re-run into a T-7, slap it on, and hold them on Ragged Hound without exciting suspicion until he could get them into the brakes and re-work the mark, couldn't he?" Peep suggested quietly. "And after he had the stuff there and re-branded it Flying Spear he could trail them across into Dakota, ship them, and prove who he was with a lease to the Flying Spear tucked in his pants pocket?"

"Hell! He might do that," Hamby admitted sourly. "But—say, how the devil do you know so much about all this if you aren't tied in on the deal, anyway?"

"Because Binder made one mistake." A grim smile moved Peep's lips. "I jumped a herd he was working on Surprise Creek. He'd run part of the brands into T-7's. Thinking in his big-headed way that he was smart and everybody else dumb, he'd started to re-work the T-7's into Flying Spears. That herd I jumped—" He whirled on Binder, who recoiled. "I scared you off, Binder, and there is no use in you denying it. That herd was the dangdest mixed-up mess of critters you ever saw. Every fresh-branded T-7 cow had a Flying Spear calf licking a new brand."

"I wasn't the only one in on that," Binder roared. "If I'm going to be railroaded, I'm squealing here and now. Squealing so that the rest of them—"

In a single bound Peep was before him to stand spread-legged, his steely eyes balls of fire in the flickering light. "You mean you're trying to squeal, jasper," he rasped out. "Trying to! But by the time I get through with you—make you confess to all your lousy lies—your word won't be worth anything on the Satanka. Even under oath in court! You did this stuff—you're taking the stretch—you, and your men, posing as Flying Spear punchers."

"Tommy helped me," Binder shouted. "Your own brother—"

Peep's attitude was dramatic. He let a clock-tick pass, a clock-tick without breath or motion. The group stood rigid as stone, waiting, watching. Then quietly: "Just what the hell would Tommy be helping you for, Binder?"

"He was turning the T-7 stuff over to me to brand Flying Spear, that's what he was doing," Binder yelled.

"So that's the play, is it?" Hamby smirked.

"What of it?" With a glance Peep silenced the thoroughly frightened Tommy. "You were branding Flying Spear for him, huh?" He paused, his swiftly functioning mind casting about desperately for some way to answer Binder's damning accusations. He found it in another lie, which he pounced on to carry him through this crisis that for the moment threatened to disrupt his plan for aiding his brother. "So you thought you had the goods on Tommy, huh?" he smiled. "You didn't know that he was grading up Jim's herds by weeding out the scrub stuff, huh? You didn't know that Jim Thompson and the O'Day brothers are partners in the Flying Spear?"

Hamby's face fell. Tommy's fearful expression faded, to be replaced by one of eager expectancy. The doctor leaned forward to hang onto every word. Binder—

"You're a dirty liar!" he ground through set teeth. Not at Peep, who faced him squarely. But at Tommy, who fell suddenly to trembling violently. "You told me—"

"I heard every word he told," Peep shot into the momentary silence. "Heard every word he told you up in the cabin that night you were so damned sure I was in jail in Satanka. You tried your best to get him to steal from Jim Thompson. He was laughing up his sleeve at you. Paying you out rope to hang yourself. You're just a sheep, Binder, on a real cow range. Do you know what that means? You've just been made a sucker of—that's all. Those T-7 critters Tommy was turning over to you belonged to him, Jim Thompson, and Peep O'Day."

"Hold on there," Thompson put in savagely. "They didn't—"

"This is once you haven't any put-in, Jim." Peep whirled on the cowman, who again had managed to elude the doctor's grasp and sat bolt upright in bed. "I've cleared you of the murder of that jasper which had been worrying the life out of you. If you've got an ounce of guts, give me a chance to clear myself. Here." He tossed the mortgage he had taken up from the two commission men onto the bed. "Read that while we finish this arguing, will you?"

Thompson glared at him angrily through glazed eyes. But a single glance at the papers smothered his rage. He started to speak, swallowed hard, lay back down to stare in open-mouthed amazement.

"So I reckon that's just about all there is to it, Bud," Peep was saying carelessly. "There's no mystery to it—never has been. It's just that you as a wide-awake, crime-ferreting sheriff, got to looking for hard ways to figure this thing out. I'm swearing to a warrant against Hi Binder for murder, rustling, and trying to kill Jim Thompson. Peep O'Day is the name to sign to that warrant in case you've forgotten it. And if you want to do a little bit of real arresting, instead of following blind trails, Binder has a crew of gunmen and rustlers. They are up in Jim Thompson's line camp in a canyon east of the Spear right now. The same cabin they took Doc to that day they kidnaped him to fix up a wounded jasper. Recollect? But you shag this Binder on into Satanka to jail. I've got plenty of posses out there in those Satanka ranches. They'll be r'aring to ride after the rest of the gang long before you get started."

"Mebbeso you've got the goods on this jasper, Peep," Hamby said, obviously crestfallen. "But I'm signing the complaint with your name. Mebbeso I've done wrong by suspecting you, but you've got to admit you haven't just played on the square. You didn't come clean by a long ways. What's a sheriff to do or think in this damned country when he plays a lone hand? There's only one thing I can't understand. That is, why did Binder go to all the trouble of branding a T-7 if he could run a critter's brand into a Flying Spear?"

"You ain't the only rancher who will ask that question," Peep answered enigmatically. "And that's just why he did it. It was done to throw you off the trail—make the stockmen suspect somebody else until he got the stuff off the range." Peep found himself praying fervently that the flimsy excuse would satisfy the slow-witted officer.

"I didn't brand T-7," Binder snarled. "Don't worry—this will all come out later—they'll find out that you're lying. Lying to frame me to save that yaller squirt." He jerked a gnarled thumb toward the ashen-faced Tommy. "I was getting every head of that T-7 stuff from your brother. You know it, damn you."

"And Tommy had the right to turn it over to you—as lessee of the Flying Spear—because it belonged to him and me," Peep lied again.

"We can figure all that out later," Hamby put in authoritatively. "It's only minor detail stuff. We've got the jasper we want. Thanks to you, Peep. And I'm much obliged. We'll nab the rest of them as soon as I can get back." He jabbed Binder roughly in the ribs with his forty-five. "Get along, you coyote," he snarled. Binder shot him a hateful glance. But with no alternative in the face of the threatening gun, he spun about. They passed outside. The door banged behind him.

After the two were gone Tommy stood by waiting nervously. Peep strode over to Jim's side. The doctor had captured a wrist, had a finger on a racing pulse. Peep looked up suddenly to face Hope, who had slipped into the room without a sound.

Their glances met, clashed. His fell away. He mopped his forehead, backed off to sink into a chair.

"Run on out for a minute, please," he pleaded with her. "There's one more thing I want to say to Jim and Tommy. Then—you might make me a cup of coffee, if it isn't too much trouble. But then—never mind—I'll get some in Satanka."

Her answer was to come quickly to his side. "I'm glad, Peep," she whispered, giving his arm a quick squeeze.

"Glad for what?" He blinked up into her eyes.

"Glad you're cleared."

"You heard?"

"Every word. You forgot to shut the door. All the ranchers were outside listening."

"Did Hamby get started to town with Binder all right?" He felt he had to ask something. He came to his feet.

"Certainly. With a posse of about ten armed men with him. But why?"

"Nothing." His shoulders sagged wearily. "Only if him and that posse ever get Binder to jail they're plumb lucky. Please—go along now, won't you, like a good—"

"Like a good girl." She made a wry face. "I've heard it ever since I can remember, Peep. Like a good girl. I'm not—"

"Oh, yes, you are," he told her fiercely. "And I—I— Please get out of here."

Chapter Twenty-Seven

THE O'DAY WAY

SHE CAST HIM A HURT LOOK. Then she turned and slowly went outside. Peep followed her and closed the door. Then he walked over and sat down on the edge of Thompson's bed.

"Jim," he said, striving to capture the cowman's roving gaze, "you gave me a raw deal—a hell of a raw deal if you want my opinion. You had to make somebody the goat. But why did you have to pick on me? You weren't fooling me any. I knew the way you flared up when those six head of calves disappeared before the round-up that something was wrong. It was all right for the other ranchers to lose critters—that didn't cost the T-7 nothing—but when rustlers started working on your stuff that was different, wasn't it? For all your slick talk you wised me up right then and there. Set me to thinking. And you were just a little too quick on those reward notices you posted in the Jumbo in Satanka. So I'm calling your hand. You offered a thousand bucks for the rustlers. I reckon you owe me a thousand, Jim, 'cause I caught 'em—dead to rights—but we'll let it ride. Even though I did catch Binder—"

He got to his feet to start pacing about nervously.

"If you'll tell me one thing: what were you doing up at the cabin in the canyon the night you had the scrap, after telling me you were going up the Belle Fourche river?"

"I just—I got caught in the storm—got twisted—" Jim stammered.

"You're lying!" Peep stopped his pacing to face the cowman, who avoided his accusing eyes. "You drove stolen cattle in there—into that line camp you built without telling a living soul—not expecting to find Binder. Come clean, Jim. That's what you built that camp for. And you didn't dare tell me, because you knew I was a square-shooter. You shot that jasper in the fracas that night! You didn't dare squeal on Binder because you thought he had the goods on you. It just happened I got hold of one of their horses that night—I wasn't following you—the horse did that, of his own accord. Packed Hope and me towards that canyon—I was hunting way out for her when—"

"Is that where she was?" Jim groaned. "My God, does she know?"

"Only that you shot a jasper. She heard that at the Flying Spear. The two of us were there when you made a getaway. But—she doesn't know it is you that is swinging a long rope, Jim. And so help me God, she's never going to know it—even if I have to take the stretch somehow. Why did you do it?"

The anger that had flared high in Thompson's eyes vanished slowly. His glance roved around like that of a trapped beast. He suddenly was an old man, crushed and beaten, the weight of years and worry indelibly stamped on his haggard face.

"I had to meet—had to meet that mortgage," he whimpered. "That mortgage you took up for me, Peep. God knows it has tormented the life out of me." Once started, it seemed to relieve him to blurt out the truth. He sat up in bed despite the doctor's efforts to hold him down.

"I got into the thing knee-deep, and I didn't seem to be able to pull out. Binder got to stealing from me as fast as I rustled from the other ranchers. I knew he was doing it, but I didn't dare squeal—not until tonight did I know I hadn't killed that walloper. I tell you I didn't dare holler. I've been through hell, Peep. Wanting to go straight—trying to quit—hoping and praying for a break so as not to ruin Hope's life. You don't know what I've suffered. But it's all over now—I'm ready to take my medicine."

"Why did you try to make them believe I shot you when you knew it was Binder?" Peep demanded brutally.

"Because everyone was suspecting you. After that gun-play in Satanka, they figured you'd slipped back to the days when— I figured I could frame you and get a new start. God forgive me, I knew it was a lousy trick, Peep. You'd always played square with me—I know it—and I tried to poison them against you, that day you called me a liar. I've sure given you a raw deal—I'm ashamed to look you in the eye—I don't deserve anything—but I'm willing to do anything to square myself if there's a chance."

"I reckon you'll have to square yourself before we get through, Jim," Peep said grimly. "Not as far as I'm concerned, but there's somebody. I've lied for you and Tommy so much I can't keep track of all the lies I've told—and some of those lies are going to take a heap of tall explaining to cover up. Especially the ones about Binder branding T-7, and us three being partners in the Flying Spear."

"You didn't have to lie for me," Tommy, once again seemingly sure of his ground, put in sneeringly. "I haven't done anything. "

"Haven't done anything!" Peep exploded. "Why you—you yaller-bellied cur, you're guilty as hell. Guilty of everything! It was you and Jim, not Hi Binder, who swung a long rope and handled that hot T-7 iron. Do you think I'm a fool? I've known it from the start, ever since I found your hair rope yonder beside a smothered chip fire on Ragged Hound. Why you lousy, lying— And you're worse than Jim. Jim stole for himself—to pull out of a pinch—you, you yaller-bellied bullfrog, stole—then sold out to Binder."

"Is that how Binder was getting my stuff?" Thompson groaned. "You dirty—"

"You ain't so lily white yourself that you can start slinging any mud, Jim," Peep suggested grimly. "We'd just better stick together. As far as the two of you are concerned, you're both dirty, lying, stealing whelps. But we've got to protect Hope! Damn your souls, if you think for a minute that clean, innocent kid is going to be dragged into this—I'll kill you both before— The only reason I'm sticking by you is to protect her!" he hurled at Thompson. "Cover you up so she won't know what a lying, thieving hound—"

"And you," he spun back on Tommy, "I promised Paw I'd look out for you—you howling, sneaking— And I'm going to do it! Although it's all the same as saddle gall to me. But there are things in life that you've got to cover up—cover up from folks who would judge you, hang you if they knew. But there's higher judges than the folks here on the Satanka. Mebbeso I've done wrong, but I'm carrying this case plumb up to Him.

"Damn you both, you sneaking, lousy rustlers—I'm only asking forgiveness for being associated with you—for being the instrument that covered up your crime. You'd both hang if I said the word. But I can't. There's an innocent life that would be ruined on account of you. A wonderful, sweet girl. You—"

He strode over to Thompson's desk. "All my life I've given you the best of things, Tommy," he rasped out. "I've threatened to quit a good many times, but somehow I always hang on and take another wallop. But now—I'm through. You'll make amends or you'll go to jail."

"For God's sake, Peep, don't send me to jail!" Tommy begged. "I know you've got the stuff on me—there's no use denying it. Binder made me double-cross Jim. He got me drunk that time at the Jumbo or I wouldn't have lost that thousand—wouldn't have stolen those six calves that got Jim all r'iled up. Losing that money at poker—a thousand dollars—I was so deep in I couldn't pull out. I've been through hell, too, Peep. Help me. I'm your brother —I'll swear to you that I'll never pack another rope—I'll do anything you ask."

"How much split have you had out of him?" Peep demanded scathingly.

"About five hundred bucks."

"Have you got it?"

"Every cent. Somehow I didn't have the heart to— It's down at the bunkhouse. Do you want me to—"

"Get it. And shake a leg coming back."

Obviously glad of the chance to escape, Tommy ducked through the door. Peep started pacing about, twisting another cigaret. Lighting it, he sucked it nervously. A short time later Tommy burst back into the room, white-faced and trembling.

"They've hung Binder," he blurted out breathlessly.

"Hung him!" Peep and Thompson shouted. "Who— where—what the—"

"The Vigilantes—took him away from Hamby—strung him up at the Ragged Hound corrals. Hamby's gone on to town to organize a new posse. One of the boys told me down to the bunkhouse." He slumped into a chair. "For God's sake, Peep, help us—or they'll do that to us, too."

"You ought to have thought of that before," Peep snapped back. "I'm plumb sorry for Binder. But he had it coming, and his going helps us. He's the only jasper who could have given testimony that would have stuck you and Jim. Did you bring that money?"

"Yes," Tommy whimpered, starting up to toss down a money bag.

"Sit down." He wilted into the chair Peep pulled over to the desk. "Write Jim Thompson a check for six thousand dollars."

Tommy stared dully at the checkbook Peep produced and smoothed out before him. "Six thousand dollars," he gasped. "I can't write a check for anything—let alone for six thousand—"

"Write a check for six thousand," Peep snapped. "It's what you're worth—every cent on earth—and it's giving you a chance to square up. It's the way Paw would have done it. And I know he wants—"

With palsied fingers Tommy scrawled the check—to Cash.

"Now fix up some sort of bill of sale to the Flying Spear and every hoof on it for Jim," Peep ordered. "Date it the day Paw died."

"But—but—" Tommy protested, "I don't understand—"

"You'll understand a hell of a sight more if the law moves down on you. I'm covering you up—you and Jim Thompson. Write it, damn you, or I'll—"

Mechanically Tommy did as he was bid. When he had finished his scratching, Peep too signed the crude instrument, picked up the money bag and handed them, along with the check, to the bewildered Thompson.

"Tommy went bad, Jim," Peep said grimly. "It's the O'Day way to try and square things. I took up that mortgage of yours with my half of the money Paw left. We're busted—but we're better off knowing we came clean. It will pull you out; then, if you figure we've got—"

Old Jim broke down. Tears trickled unheeded across his wrinkled cheeks.

"I ain't deserving of this—after the way I've treated you, Peep," he sobbed. "Keep it! Money can't pay for those rustled cows."

"The hell it can't," Peep shot out. "Figure, you idiot. With Binder gone, nobody but us three knows who handled that T-7 iron. Get a tally from the ranchers of every head they've lost. Binder sold part of them. But we can tell them we found every hoof. We'll pay them back in Spear stuff as far as it will go. Then we'll run T-7's into Spears to make up for the rest of them. They'll never need to know that you and Tommy rustled."

"Peep." Thompson was sobbing loudly, a queer horrible sound from the lips of a stern-faced man. "What are you doing this for?"

"For—" Peep's hesitancy was noticeable, "for Tommy. I promised Paw—promised him I'd be his keeper. I'm trying to live up to the name."

"You're a white man." Thompson choked. "But it's too much to ask—too much of a sacrifice to pull me out of the mess I've gotten myself into. I—" He wiped his eyes savagely with the back of a horny hand. "You told Hamby us three were pards—"

"Just lying some more—for Tommy's sake," Peep said hotly. "I had to explain those T-7's Tommy was turning over to Binder."

"But—supposing they catch you up. Supposing they—"

"I reckon they will if things break as they usually do," Peep responded grimly. "But I've developed into the best single-handed liar on this range—or on any other for that matter."

"Hand me that pen and ink and some paper," Thompson ordered brokenly. "As long as everybody else has taken to writing, I reckon I'll just do a little myself. I started Tommy to swinging a long rope—don't blame him, Peep —but he double-crossed me because he got into a pinch like I was in." He broke off to write steadily for a few minutes.

"I reckon we're even now. This here money of Tommy's and yours—paying off that mortgage clears me for a while. The stuff I've shipped will take care of the rest of the paper that is pressing. I'll get a tally, like you said, and we'll make good every rustled critter. Here, Peep— it's for you and Tommy." Peep took the paper the cowman handed him and rammed it in his pocket without so much as glancing at it.

"I'm all in now," old Jim muttered, sinking back onto his pillow.

"And so am I," Tommy murmured. "If you don't mind I'll stretch out here on the floor. I don't know when I've been so tired. God, I'm glad it's all over, Jim. I—"

"The coffee you ordered is waiting, Mister O'Day," Hope's voice broke in on the suddenly silent group, from the other room.

Peep started away. Tommy halted him, with outstretched hand.

"Peep," he said earnestly, "you're all right—a real white man. I'm shooting square with you from now on, like Paw wanted. "

Peep gripped the outstretched hand warmly. "I knew it was in you somewhere, kid," he said soberly. "You wouldn't be an O'Day unless you had some white. That hair rope—the one you left beside those rustled critters—it's on my saddle. I reckon you understand now that it isn't quite long enough yet to cover the whole Satanka."

There were tears in Tommy's eyes as he spun about and went outside, closing the door softly behind him.

Hope joined Peep. Avoiding her inquisitive gaze, he sat down and sipped a cup of steaming coffee that she had poured for him. Recalling suddenly the paper Jim had given him, he pulled it from his pocket and read it. Then without a word he passed it over to her.

"Why, Peep," she exclaimed excitedly, hovering near him. "Jim has given you and Tommy each a third interest in all his holdings—a third interest in the big T-7. Isn't that wonderful?"

"Mebbeso." He shrugged. "But it is taking it away from you when Jim goes on."

"Mebbe not." She mocked his serious tone. "You can't always tell."

He leaped to his feet, faced her. "What do you mean?" he demanded huskily. "Are you and Tommy figuring—"

"I should say not." There was real scorn in her voice.

"I thought mebbeso." His shoulders sagged wearily. "From the way you spoke I figured you were aiming to team—"

"I am some day," she remarked lightly. "With all my heart. Every girl figures that some day she'll—"

"But us getting this interest in the T-7 will take it away

from you," he said again. "Unless you are figuring on marrying Tommy."

"How is that?" she asked, her gaze falling and a flush creeping to the roots of her hair. "There are two of you O'Days, aren't there?"

A dull flush spread over his own face.

"Hope!" His voice was strained, unnatural. "There are two of us O'Days. You don't mean, honest to God, Hope —you don't—"

"Peep O'Day," she said angrily, stamping her foot, "are you absolutely blind? Does a cyclone have to hit you to make you see anything? I'm disgusted! Even when I was doubting you, why didn't you—oh, Peep, why didn't you take me in your arms? Peep, I love you! Can't you see—it isn't Tommy—it never has been! If you don't take me, Peep—"

"Well, I'll be darned," he blurted out. "You don't mean—"

"I don't mean anything." She smiled through a blinding flood of happy tears, bending over him. "Won't you have another cup of coffee, Mister O'Day? And I don't mean—Tommy, either. And with that cup of coffee, Mister O'Day—would you please kiss your hostess—"

Peep blinked and turned on her his eyes that were glazed with surprise.

"Kiss my hostess?" he repeated blankly. "Are you asking me— Hope, do you really mean after all these years of waiting, hoping that you—you want me to—"

"After all these years, you silly! Why didn't you try to defend yourself? After all these years! I've loved you always, Peep. Peep, hold me close—squeeze me tight—I need it, Peep—I— Wait, you're choking me! But go ahead, Peep, I love it."

Francis W. Hilton was born in Lexington, Nebraska, but at two years of age moved with his family to Newcastle, Wyoming, where his father worked for the *Newcastle News-Journal*, a newspaper he eventually bought. Newspaper journalism was in Hilton's blood, and after attending a year at the University of Michigan he returned to Newcastle where he worked for his father. In Newcastle, Hilton covered the sheriff's office and got to know several prisoners who told him stories of the old West in the days of cattle wars and outlaws. These stories inspired his ambition to write Western fiction, which he began publishing in the 1920s in such pulps as *Western Story Magazine*, *Frontier Stories*, and *Lariat Story Magazine*. Beginning with *Phantom Rustlers* in 1934, Hilton branched out into writing Western novels. Some of these such as *Long Rope* (1935) were expansions of short stories that had earlier appeared in magazines. In most of Hilton's stories, there are elements of mystery and detection, thus combining one popular genre with another. Hilton's descriptions of Western terrain and natural occurrences such as cloudbursts are extremely vivid and unforgettable. In the 1940s, while still writing Western fiction for the magazine market, Hilton continued working for various local newspapers as a writer and editor, and in 1947 founded the *Columbia Basin News* in the state of Washington. In the 1950s, Hilton bought a magazine intended for vegetarians, and helped by his wife, published it until he retired in 1959. His last days found him living again in Newcastle. His reputation as a Western author rests primarily on the ten novels he wrote, many of which were subsequently published in paperback editions, and all of which, in Hilton's words, provide a whiff of something "that reminded me of sagebrush."